MOON STRUCK

ENKAY D DURAND

Copyright © ENKay D Durand, 2007

All rights reserved by the author(s). No part of this publication can be reproduced, stored in a retrieval system, or transmitted in any form or by any method or means, electronic, mechanical, photocopying, recording or otherwise, without the prior permission of the publishers and/or authors.

Terra Press Publishing
608 Rugby Road, Brooklyn, NY 11230
Visit our Web site at www.terrapresspublishing.com

While every precaution has been taken in the preparation of this book, Terra Press Publishing assumes no responsibilities for errors or omissions, or for damages resulting from the use of information contained herein. The appearance and contents of this book are the sole responsibility of the author.

This book is a work of fiction. The people, places and events portrayed in this book are a product of the author's imagination. Any similarity to person(s) living or dead is purely coincidental and was not intended by the author.

Library of Congress Control Number: 2007923678

Durand D ENKay

Moon Struck: ENKay D Durand, 1st edition

ISBN 978-0-6154-3974-6

10 9 8 7 6 5 4 3 2

Cover Design: Regina Brown

Printed in the United States of America

Terra Press Enterprises, Inc

If you brought this book without a cover you should be aware that this book is stolen property. It was reported as "unsold and destroyed" to the publisher and neither the author nor the publisher has received any payment for this "stripped book."

Dedication

I would like to thank my mom Ellie, Rocky D, Ricky T, Andrea J, Dr. Dave Cook, Chuck B, and most of all my four children for encouraging and helping me along the way. For believing in me when I had difficulties believing in myself. As well as Regina Brown, my editor who believed in my story and helped made it come to life. Also M, who worked and paid the bills giving me the time to write. Thank you.

Chapter 1
LIFE'S WOES AND GOALS

She's *weird*!" Noelle said, flipping her hair and sneering as she turned to face Kyra; her eyes cold and hard. "I wouldn't be surprised if she tried to kill us all. You know she's crazy."

Shannon, stealing a quick glance towards Kyra put a finger up to her thin lips and whispered, "Shhh. She's going to hear you."

Then, as if a cork had popped from a bottle, both girls broke out in giggles. Kyra's heart sank. *Why can't they just leave me alone,* she thought, as she continued her trek down the hall towards class. Noelle and Kyra use to be friends over the summer when Kyra had first moved to the area.

Noelle's usual friends had gone away for the summer or were busy with summer jobs. So Noelle befriended Kyra to keep herself busy until school started; then she dumped her like a used wad of gum. Kyra hadn't thought she told Noelle anything that could be used negatively against her, but once school started, Noelle and her friends had found a way.

Kyra had to admit that she admire their ability to turn the most positive into something horribly negative.

"Loser," Noelle and Shannon said, walking briskly around her, knocking her roughly into a wall as they passed.

Kyra wanted to be invisible. She wanted to be somewhere else, anywhere but there. Her mother told her that she just needed to deal with it; that high school was a learning process and that kids can be cruel, but in the adult world it was different. Kyra knew her mother hadn't given her all the facts. Not about the learning process or the fact that kids can be cruel, but of the adult world being different. The adult world was filled with just as many cruelties. But it wasn't as blatant. It was just a bit more polite, more lies. She remembered listening to her mother having a talk with one of the neighbors about how the outside faucet handle went missing.

"I can't believe anyone would steal a faucet handle," the neighbor said. "It was probably just a prank. You know how kids are these days."

Kyra's mother just smiled and nodded; waving goodbye as the neighbor left. Her eyes filled with sadness because she knew that Kyra had seen the neighbor steal the faucet handle.

"Mom," Kyra said, somewhat perturbed. "Why didn't you say anything to her? Don't you believe me? I saw her take it!"

"Yes dear. I believe you. I can always pick up another handle."

Kyra couldn't believe her ears. Her mother knew the neighbor had lied and was letting her get away with it! During the course of a month, Kyra watched in silence as every new handle her mom bought continued to disappear.

She felt hopeless watching her mother's sadness constantly grow. Kyra just couldn't stand by and watch her mother suffer silently, so she decided to tell her father. When she told her father what was happening, he just shook his head and said that he had more important matters to deal with. Then he'd walk into his office and close the door—shutting her out. The same way he shut her mother out of his life years ago; he would sooner sit in solitude rather than to take time out of his busy schedule to explain the logistics of his career in the military; he found other people to talk to, people who understood how the military worked without having to explain everything to her mother.

Her father went to all the military functions by himself. When Kyra's mother expressed wanting to go with him, he'd shrug his shoulders and usually say, "You wouldn't have any fun there anyways. The last time I brought you there you embarrassed me. Remember? You had the nerve to ask who they were."

"But I didn't know who they were," she'd offer, in her defense. "You didn't tell me."

"What you asked them was rude. Besides, I only have one ticket anyways—got to go—bye."

Then out the door he'd go, off into the night, alone once more. Kyra's mother was lost in a world she did not fully understand and would probably never know; her father would be retiring soon and Kyra guessed that it didn't matter anymore whether her mother understood his world or not.

What she did understand was the solitude of being on the outside looking into a world she was suppose to be apart of and wasn't. Even adults weren't protected from the callousness of the world.

"Miss. Davis," the biology teacher, Mr. Wilson said, stirring her out her daydream. "Are you with us?"

"Uh—yes. Mr. Wilson," she answered.

"Well, pay attention. I was asking, what are the differences between viruses and bacteria?"

Kyra could only stare at Mr. Wilson dumbfounded. She hadn't been paying attention to what was going on in class.

"Day dreaming again I see. Well, instead of day dreaming maybe you should spend more time studying. Do you think that is possible Miss. Davis?"

"Yes," she whispered, solemnly.

She nodded her head, somewhat embarrassed, trying to ignore the snickers from the class.

"Now class, can anyone here, beside Miss Davis, give me the answer to that question?"

Kyra could only see the pages of her biology book as the glistening droplets fell and burst upon its pristine pages and she hoped that no one else notice. The bell finally rang for her next class. Kyra sat with her head down on the desk, watching feet scurry by around her. She blinked when she noticed large black spoke rubber wheels, edged by a smooth black inner rim, pull up to where she was sitting. She kept her head buried on her desk, but she was still able to see denim clad legs, topped off by footed white cross trainers, sitting on metal supports.

"Hey," a voice gently permeated her thoughts. "Don't let Mr. Wilson, or the rest of those jerks intimidate you."

Kyra couldn't believe her ears; she wanted to put a face to the whimsical voice, with a slight Scandinavian accent. She raised her head slowly and was delighted at what her eyes had gazed upon. His face was smooth and cream colored; it glowed like the remnants of some far off star. His hair was dark brown and his eyes beamed a deep golden brown that reminded her of warm caramel lightly dipped in dark chocolate. Mmmm...the thought of chocolate was all she could think about.

"Hello," he said, gallantly. "Aaron Larsen, at your service."

Then he bowed in his wheelchair with an exaggerated sweep of his arm.

Ah, hi. I'm Kyra Davis. I haven't seen you in class before?"

"I just transferred into this class. You know the prerequisites for college and all."

Kyra smiled to herself.

Maybe this school wasn't so bad after all, she thought. Just maybe there really was a balance in the world.

Kyra understood college. She told Aaron about attending a summer writing course, last year before moving, at a local college in Virginia. She loved every minute of it, writing to her hearts content. She had even started to think that maybe for a career she would become a journalist and from there try her hand at writing fantasies. She could have kept on talking had it not been for the one-minute warning bell, vibrating through the air, startling them both and interrupting their conversation. Kyra stood there wishing they could go on talking forever.

"Well," Aaron said sweetly as he rolled off to his next class. "See you later."

Kyra couldn't help turning around. She watched him maneuver effortlessly through the horde of people until he disappeared into the mist of her memories.

After school, Aaron was waiting for Kyra by the bus stop. When he spotted her he waved his arms wildly to get her attention. Kyra saw Aaron waving and she walked over to meet him. She liked the idea that anyone cared enough to wait for her after school.

"Hey Kyra," Aaron said, grinning. Then he popped an impressive wheelie in her direction. "Need a lift?"

A lift, Kyra thought. What was he talking about? Did he mean for her to sit on his lap? Aaron's face was gleaming, just as it had been when she first met him in the classroom. It made Kyra wonder if he always smiled and perhaps maybe he was only this smiley for her.

"You're just the person I've been waiting to see," he said, his smile fading a little. "We have a lot to talk about."

Kyra stood there, one hand gripping her backpack and the other on her hip.

"Really? Oh, and by the way, I don't need a lift. I have a bus to catch."

"Do you think you could meet me at Barkers Island tonight?" he said hypnotically, his eyes gazing into hers. "It's very important."

"Ya," she answered, hastily. "I guess that might be okay. What time?"

"How about seven?"

"Well, I have curfew at ten, but seven sounds okay."

"Great! Meet me by the old whaleback ship, at seven, on Barkers Island."

"Okay. See you then."

Aaron rolled off down the street popping wheelies and whistling. Kyra stood at the bus stop and watched him. He had put some kind of spell on her.

What was I thinking, she thought. Scolding herself on the bus ride home. She barely knew the guy and here she was planning to meet with him at night in a secluded place. What would her mother think? That thought stayed with her on the ride home. She sat on the bus staring out the window; somehow she felt drawn to Aaron. She decided right there and then that she had to go; not just to find out what was so important, but to find out why she was so mysteriously drawn to him.

Chapter 2
THE TELLING

Kyra Gertrude Davis was born four weeks early on a frosty evening in late November. Her mother and father, thrilled by the birth of their first child, couldn't wait to bring Kyra home. She was a thin baby, with rather long feet that stood out like a fire in the dark. She had jet-black hair that spiked across the top of her perfectly shaped head and her eyes were sharp and alert. Gooing and cooing as both her parents took turns snuggling her into their loving arms. Once home her mother and father discovered that Kyra was a sunny baby true to her name, but with a strong stubborn streak that often frustrated them; refusing certain foods, sleeping and untimely diaper changes.

Her first home was a quaint, sunny yellow, three bedroom military house located on Whiteman Air Force Base in Missouri. Her father was a career military person and her mother stayed home to care for Kyra. At five months old she was a chubby toddler crawling and using her new mobility to discover what dust bunnies, wiggling worms and rocks covered in mud tasted like; reveling and giggling at each new discovery. By the time she reached nine months old she was walking and running. She refused to wear shoes because she loved how the blades of grass tickled her toes and the cool mashing of the soil when she walked or ran. When her mother brought her to the playground she'd climb and swing as graceful and unimpeded as a monkey in its jungle home.

She had plenty of friends that lived in neighboring houses so there was always someone to play with. When she turned three, she could read small chapter books and do basic addition and subtraction. Her parents face beamed with pride watching her use her newly developed academic skills. She often read stories to her friends and tried to teach them to add using candy. Her young life was filled with the warmth and security of two loving and encouraging parents who never told her she couldn't achieve anything if she put her mind to it.

When Kyra reached school age, they moved from Missouri to North Dakota. While her parents seemed elated by this move, Kyra's stomached ached and tears flowed at the thought of leaving her home. When they were settled in North Dakota, her mother decided on home schooling Kyra instead of sending her to kindergarten. She was the only child in the neighborhood that was home schooled. She often felt left out and isolated when the other children in the neighborhood talked about public school; riding the big yellow bus and their lunches served on trays.

The other children told her it would be great to be able to do their schoolwork in pajamas and eat whatever they wanted for lunch instead of being stuck with whatever was on the menu. Kyra would laugh and enjoy the attention and acceptance from her peers and the isolation that cast a shadow inside her, would blow away into the wind. She loved spending time learning with her mother, playing and being together. Her father, it always seemed, was gone on trips or working at the office.

Kyra did not lack the socialization that many children and adults assumed she did because she was home schooled, but gained the ability to pick and choose her own peer group rather than have to settle in a caste system that many normal schools have. This gave Kyra the freedom to find herself, her own style and learn at her own rate. She was able to take the day off when she wanted to and go sightseeing with her mother. Wherever they moved, there were always other home schooled children around; one just needed to know where to look. There were also groups of home schooler's who willingly welcomed them into their groups. The only socialization Kyra lacked was by choice, her choice. Not some strangers telling her to do so. Kyra's parents sent her to high school because they felt that it would be beneficial to her to get to know the other side, as they put it. Call it a learning curve if you will. But Kyra felt, if this was the other side they could have it; she didn't want it!

Kyra arrived home at her usual time and finished her schoolwork well before dinner. She and her mother, Sunny, usually ate dinner together without her father present. His working hours were usually so erratic that it was almost impossible for them to plan meals together as a family.

And that night was no exception.

"Kyra?" Her mother asked, while they ate. "You said you were going out tonight?"

"Uhm, ya. To meet this guy I met at school today. His name is Aaron and he's, well, I'm supposed to meet him tonight."

"Why isn't he picking you up?" Her mother asked suspiciously. "And where are you going to have this, talk?"

"Oh mom, you know how it is," she pleaded. "We're just meeting at one of the usual hangouts to talk about school. He's really nice. I think you'd like him. In fact, he seems like the kind of guy you would have probably dated."

Her mother took a swig of coffee and paused; Kyra could almost see the wheels swirling in her head. She placed her cup on a saucer and gazed at Kyra unblinking.

"Better yet, I would like to meet him," she said. "Where does he live?"

"I—I don't know where he lives. I didn't ask him."

"Well, I suggest you find out."

"Oh, please mom, I finally made a friend. Usually it takes me until just before we move to make a friend. You've always trusted my judgment..."

Her mother held up her hand and Kyra stop in mid sentence. She knew the rules; it meant for her to stop speaking and listen. Her mother picked up her cup of coffee and held it in the air.

"Just don't let your father find out I let you go without very much information. Here, take my cell phone and if anything comes up call me. Okay? I just want to keep you safe."

Their hand's touched briefly when she reached for the phone. Kyra and her mother smiled as their eyes met, conveying between them an unspoken understanding. It was the kind of understanding only a mother and daughter knew.

"I promise to call ASAP if needed and I won't take any chances. Thanks mom. I love you."

"I love you too."

Kyra jumped up from her chair and paused at the kitchen door.

"Don't make me regret this," her mother said.

She turned around and looked at her mother, still sitting at the table, holding her beloved coffee cup.

"I won't," she replied.

"Well I'm off to finish my homework," her mother said.

Sunny looked at least ten years younger than her age. Her hair was the color of wheat in autumn, with no signs of graying, and her eyes were the color of a dark aquamarine sea that shifted in the light. When she told people she was finally starting college after spending sixteen years at home they applauded her. She knew many women her age that had degrees and careers that paid good money. Sunny had given up the career path for a job that had no income, vacations, or days off. It was a continuous job she worked 24/7, but it came with a reward that was priceless. She was a caretaker; she stayed home and took care of her family.

"I'm proud of you mom," Kyra said. "I know it can't be easy."

Sunny sighed deeply, and gave a little half smile.

"It's the military part that's the most difficult Kyra. Like the old adage says, if the military wanted you to have it they would have issued it and no they don't issue families."

Kyra blew her mom a kiss and laughed when she reached out to grab it. Then she pretended to place the kiss on her cheek. Kyra glimpse at the clock; it was 6:10 PM.

I better get ready to go, she thought.

She wondered why she agreed to meet this strange boy in the first place. Then she remembered, but why the old whaleback ship? Some people said it was haunted and it wasn't exactly a place that was accessible for someone in a wheelchair. The ship was encased on the bottom by rocks and sand to stabilize it; it definitely wasn't wheelchair friendly; heck, it wasn't even foot friendly.

Kyra quickly changed into a warm sweatshirt, blue jeans and her favorite pair of cross trainers. She also made sure to carry along a flashlight, water bottle, a notebook and pen. She took one last look in the mirror to make sure every thing was in place, smoothing down her glossy hair. Then she clipped the cell phone to her jeans and she was ready to venture into the night. Barkers Island was only about a mile from her house and the ship was just a short walk from there. Kyra checked her watch and hurried towards the front door.

"Bye mom!" she yelled, walking out the door and venturing into the night.

Chapter 3
THE REALITY OF A DREAM

Kyra arrived at the ship out of breath and with thirty seconds to spare. She looked around for Aaron; he had five seconds before he would be late. Kyra was very punctual when it came to time. That's when she noticed a shadow of movement flicker against the side of the ship.

"Hello," she said. "Aaron, are you here? Is that you?"

Her reply was the sounds chickens make followed by a chorus of laughter.

"Who's there?"

Her heart was pounding in her chest like a drum; she fled from the voices towards the other side of the ship near the water's edge.

As she rounded the corner, air coming in gulps, she skidded to a stop when she saw Aaron standing in the dim moonlight; behind him were some other people as well.

"I'm sorry; I didn't mean to scare you," Aaron said, in a voice so smooth it reminded her of warm fresh cream. "Glad you could make it."

She took a few deep breaths, trying to regain her self-control, and steadied her pounding heart.

"Um, no problem Aaron," she stammered. "I just didn't expect anyone else to be here but us."

She scanned the faces of the others and noticed that they were staring at her like they were cramming for a test; studying her face, clothes, shoes—all of her! They turned and whispered to one another, barely being able to be heard over the lapping waves.

"Is he sure she's *the one*."

Kyra wondered what they were whispering about. She wiped her sweaty palms nervously against her jeans and looked to Aaron for answers.

"Aaron who are these people? I thought we were going to talk alone?"

Kyra hadn't really noticed that Aaron wasn't sitting in a wheelchair like he had been earlier at school, but standing on his own two legs. He was quite tall; towering over her by at least six inches. Kyra was shocked; she stood there with her mouth opened, swaying precariously on her feet. She felt like she was involved in some sort of prank and wanted no part of it.

"What's going on...?" was all she was able to say as the group surrounded her, stealing her oxygen. She was finding it difficult to breathe, her breath coming in hard gasps, before she melted to the ground unconscious.

"What happened?" She asked, dreamily, as she started to wake.

She was lying in the cool sand, lulled by the sound of waves washing on shore.

"Is she awake?" Someone said.

"She's starting to come around." Another replied.

Kyra's blood ran cold through her body. *What's going on*? She thought. She slid her hand slowly along her side, trying to reach the spot where she had clipped the cell phone to her pants only to find it void of phone. Her heart was beating rapidly in her chest; she sat up quickly and opened her eyes. Aaron was standing above her holding the gleaming gray phone.

"Looking for this?" he said.

"Yes," she replied, hotly.

Then she snatched the cell phone from his hand. The aroma of burning wood wafted in the air and she noticed a faint flicker in the darkness; it seemed to be firelight off into the far corner of the beach, the whaleback ship silhouetted in the dim moonlight.

"What do you want from me?" Kyra asked.

Aaron didn't answer; he reached out and offered her his hand, which she accepted somewhat reluctantly. She watched him grasp her hand and pull her to her feet.

"I was worried about you Kyra, you fainted. The others and I moved you to a softer spot away from the rocks and on the beach. We were only trying to help."

He was gesturing with his hands, palms up and arms spread innocently. Kyra looked around and saw the flames from the fire licking at the night and the quiet glow the moon cast upon the water. Aaron put a protective arm around her and guided her towards the golden glow of the fire.

The flames caressed the shadowy outline of people sitting, standing and crouching within its grasp. Aaron and Kyra walked over and sat down side by side on a large piece of driftwood. She noticed, bordered on both sides of them were at least twenty other people around the fire. Their eyes cast a strange glow that wavered off the firelight. They talked and laughed and seemed totally oblivious to Aaron and Kyra. She found herself relaxing a little as she gazed off into the twinkling moonlit night. The fire was warm and inviting.

"It's a beautiful night Aaron. Would you please tell me why you asked me to come here?"

Aaron gently grasped her by the chin and lifted her face up so that her eyes could look directly into his and he whispered one-word, "*Watch.*"

She didn't understand what he was talking about. *Watch what,* she thought, *the moon, the stars or the water. What?*

She looked around and realized that something very strange was happening. The others were beginning to change. Slowly at first, then their noses elongated, their mouths filled with sharp pointed teeth, their skin became rough and scaly, each bearing a uniquely different color. Their feet grew long and sharp and their hands where like huge talons with pointed claws on the end. Nothing Kyra had ever read, either fact or myth, prepared her for what she was witnessing. Her eyes glazed over, as she was either unwilling or unable to take her eyes off them; vibrations ran through her body, bringing her back to reality. The whole group of them roared loudly, like musicians in a symphony, signaled by a composer, right on cue. They stretched their long leathery wings and with a slight flap, producing only the slightest bit of a breeze, off they flew into the sparkling midnight blue sky.

"Aaron...!" She tried to speak, but her words were trapped in her throat, as she saw he was starting to change too.

With a loud gasp, she fell off the driftwood awestruck and horrified. The boy, the one she had known as Aaron, gingerly reached out a clawed hand towards her. His scales flashed with the color of dark rich hematite and his hulk of a body towered over her, blocking out the warm earth glow of the fire.

Wow, he's just as stunning a dragon as he is human she thought in her mind.

"Take my hand," his voice rumbled.

This must be how a rabbit feels standing next to a ravenous wolf, knowing it could be eaten at any given moment, she wondered.

It was all she could do to repel the shock she felt as she gazed up at the monstrous, sparkling, hematite colored dragon with Aaron's beautiful golden brown eyes. As if hypnotized, she lifted her arm up and reached out her hand towards his.

"Come," he said, grabbing her hand and lifting her up to her feet.

Her arms were out in front of her as Aaron led her by the hand closer to the edge of the mysterious frosty water flowing towards Lake Superior and jumped in. The frigid water permeated every part of her with the iciness of a tomb and greedily sucked up her body's vitality until she felt nothing. Though her lungs still burned with life, breathing like a fish in the frosty water, her frozen eyes could only see the blackened world around her in the lake that is known to never give up its dead.

Was I going to be one of them? She thought. *Was I going to die?*

She could see the moon glowing on the waters surface that was just beyond her reached and resolved calmly within her that this was her final destiny. The blackness ahead and below finally ebbed and a faint world gradually came into view. She looked at Aaron, the huge magnificent, boy dragon, still gripping her ghostly numb hand, tightly in his large claw and she relaxed. Kyra glimpsed at the movements of shifting shadows to the side of her, it was some of the other dragons. They were diving and darting effortlessly through the water chasing small sleek silvery silhouettes from behind. The dragons seemed to be working together. She watched amazed as one of them tossed a plump silvery figure high into the air above while the others gave chase, each taking its turn to volley the silver form until an amethyst colored dragon flew up and greedily gulped it down in mid-air. They reminded her of the Orca whales she'd seen in a documentary when she was a little girl; they worked together to capture food, then played with it before devouring it.

Who are these people, these dragons? She said to herself. *What do they want with me? Why haven't I drowned? How am I still alive?* All these questions floated through her head as her body bobbed and weaved through the murky water. She was thankful that Aaron's grip was strong. The deeper they went the less she thought and the more she allowed herself to see, feel and enjoy the independence of the characteristic restraints of her human body in deep water. She could see the bottom of the lakebed, rocks, sand and some debris. It was an alien land encompassed in shades of blacks, grays and whites.

Maybe this is what Duluth/Superior would look like on the surface if the trees and buildings all vanished from the land. She imagined.

Fish of all sizes and shapes whizzed by as they glided easily through the water, skimming the sandy bottom as they traveled along.

"Hang on tight Kyra," Aaron said, pulling her onto his back. And like a stone shot from a slingshot they rose higher and higher until—*Whoosh*—they emerged from the raw water; ascending swiftly into the starlit sky. They were *FLYING;* really flying, high above the lake, its waves rippling and dancing. The other dragons were blinking in and out from sight creating a Picasso effect as the moon reflected on its fluttering canvas. Aaron and Kyra soared over shingled slanted rooftops, gliding on the wind; the sky their playground, while the stars and moon were their audience. She did not feel cold, or wet; only the jubilation of life as the wind whisked across her body and through her chestnut hair. It was a freedom that she had never known existed before. She prodded Aaron with her hand.

"Can we go there?" she asked, pointing a stiff finger at Enger Tower as they skirted by it.

Careening sharply, she could feel the fluid pumping movements of his wings and then he landed on the very top of Enger Tower. Her breath came in sharp icy rasps as she gaped at the twinkling lights of the city that lay below them. For the first time in a long time she felt like she belonged. Once again she could hear Aaron's voice in her head.

"Stunning, isn't it."

She nodded slowly in agreement; her nose tingled, her body started to shiver and her teeth chattered in the icy wind. Aaron slid her off his back and placed her carefully on the top of the tower, by the green light, giving her something to hold on to so she would not slide off. He took a short breath and flames issued from his nostrils. *Whoosh!*

She heard a slight thrumming in her head, as an orange light engulfed her; she was to astonish to scream. The flames did not burn her, but dried her clothes and warmed her body.

"How did you do that?"

"Dragon's secret."

"Okay," she said, gazing wide eyed. "I can live with that."

Looking off into the distance she could see the others soaring through the air; the moon reflecting off the sheen of their scales. She felt like she was watching a fairy tale unfold before her very eyes, captivated by the site of it all. She wasn't ready to leave her wondrous fantasy when Aaron tapped her arm gently.

"Time to go."

When she didn't come willingly he pulled on her arm, she resisted, as she closed her eyes trying to will gravity to hold them in place. A sharp quick yank on her arm and she was airborne for only a moment before landing abruptly on Aaron's back. Then she felt a jolt as Aaron leaped into the air. The wind tugged at her clothes as she opened her eyes and watched in sadness as her amazing fantasy vanished behind her. Their flight was short, landing once again at Barkers Island by where the fire had been. Kyra jumped gracefully off Aaron's back onto the crisp sand.

"How did we do that?" she said, stammering as she watched him change back into human form.

He grinned, reached out and hugged her as she started to step away from him.

"Does it really matter?" he said with a cocky grin and eyes aglow. "You'll find out when the time is right and only then."

Time? Why does that sound familiar? She thought.

"What time is it?"

"Ten minutes to ten. You still have plenty of time."

He gazed at her face, smiling warmly, but the worried frown and creases in her face did not lessen.

"Don't worry. I'll call Andrea to give you a ride home so you won't be late."

Before she could say thank you Aaron had closed his eyes and opened them again. A large shadow loomed over them and landed. Kyra took a step back, her heart was fluttering and her mouth dry and she almost lost her footing. She was too stunned to speak as a large amethyst dragon, the one she saw eat the fish, landed beside her and instantly changed into a stunning girl with jet-black hair and eyes just as dark. In human form, she was just a little taller than Kyra with a rounded full body.

"You called?" she asked, her eyes glinting lightheartedly at Aaron.

She was relaxed and friendly; acting as if nothing out of the usual was happening and maybe for them it wasn't, but for Kyra this was all too much like a dream.

"Andrea," Aaron cooed, "could you please give Kyra a ride home for me so she's not late?"

"Sure, why not," she replied. "Follow me Kyra."

She motioned to Kyra with her hand to come. Kyra followed Andrea submissively to her car, walking like she was in a dream, apparently still mesmerized by the night's events. Kyra even forgot to say goodbye to Aaron as she left. They climbed in Andrea's small blue car, buckled their seatbelts and the engine roared to life. Andrea put the car in gear and sped away from Barkers Island and on to highway two. Kyra started to explain nervously where she lived, but before she got the chance Andrea said, "I already know."

"Really?" Kyra replied.

"Yes. I'm practically your neighbor. I live just a few blocks from you."

"Oh." Kyra sputtered, turned and stared out the front windshield.

Why haven't I seen her before tonight? Kyra thought.

"We're here," Andrea said, pulling up and stopping in front of a White house trimmed in green.

Kyra nodded numbly and climbed out of the car.

"Thanks for the ride Andrea."

"Any time," she replied. "See you tomorrow."

"Yes. Tomorrow."

Kyra closed the front door and walked zombified to her room; she grabbed her pajamas from her bed and quietly slipped into the bathroom for a long hot bath. The warm, lavender scented, bath water seeped deeply into her chilled bones, relaxing her. She lay there and closed her eyes picturing the night's events. She stayed in the tub until the water-cooled around her and pruned her skin. Feeling drowsy, she climbed out of the tub, dried herself quickly and put on her warm flannel pajamas.

"Goodnight mom," she said bumping into her mother as she emerged from the steamy bathroom.

"Did you have a good time tonight?" Her mother asked, following closely behind her into her bright blue bedroom. She stood just inside the doorway and watched Kyra climb quickly into bed.

"Um ya, I did. I'm exhausted. Goodnight mom, love you."

Her mother walked over to the bed and tucked the covers around her, then she leaned over and kissed her softly on the cheek before turning to leave, pausing at her door as if she forgot something, then turning her head over her shoulder.

"Goodnight honey, see you in the morning and then you better tell me all the details."

She shut the door as if on cue when the word 'details' was spoken. Kyra had really wanted to tell her mom everything that had happen tonight, but it seemed so unreal.

Did what I think happen really happen or did I just imagine it. She thought, snuggling deeper under her soft flannel sheets and blankets. She carefully pondered what had happened and wondered what she was going to tell her mother in the morning. Then she closed her eyes and set her mind adrift.

The way the other kids changed. All the different iridescent colors they had become and they all seemed to be able to swim as well as fly. She wondered if those kids went to her school or were they from other parts of the region. When Aaron changed into a dragon he retained the same youthfulness as when he was in human form. The small horns on top of his head, his lithe muscular body and his scales were gleaming as a newly polished hematite. She wondered if they pick their color or if they were born with it. None of them were the same color. Why were they able to change into dragons? Why here in the northland. All the fantasy novels she ever read that dealt with the myths of dragons, through Europe and Asia. She never read about dragons occupying the United States. If all what she thought and saw was true, then dragons still exist in this day and time. The dragons shape was similar to the description of how the European dragons looked; maybe they migrated here like the drones of people from Europe, Asia, Africa and South America had?

She concluded that she had to talk to Aaron and find out what and why all this was happening. Sleep enveloped her mind and body; she saw herself flying high over Lake Superior and its dancing waves; the moon and stars glittered above her, the shadowy water below; it was an eerie sight. She could almost feel the brisk icy winds on her skin, causing her to shiver at the thought. Behind her, she could see the electrical lights of the Arial Lift Bridge, sparkled off into the distance, as she flew farther away from the shores of Duluth/Superior heading up towards Canada. Somewhere in the murkiness of her mind, she thought she heard Aaron's voice calling out to her.

"*Goodnight Kyra. Sweet dreams.*"

"Goodnight Aaron," she murmured, as she flew through the icy air of her dreams.

Chapter 4
QUESTIONS AND REALITIES

Yuck, Puddily pops again?" Kyra said, wincing. "Where in the world did you find these?"

"You know when you were little Kyra," her father said. "Puddily Pops were your favorite. In fact, you use to sing that jingle all the time."

Puddily Pops is made of pudding lumps.
That's dried in nature's way.
So be sure to try Puddily Pops today.
Secreting a van-choc sugary flavor.
That wrestles on your tongue.
That's what makes Puddily Pops so much fun.
They are filled with oozy goozy goodness.

You'll want to eat them everyday.

"Dad enough! I remember the jingle, but I'm not that little girl anymore."

"Hummm..." he murmured sadly.

Her father had a difficult time remembering that Kyra was growing up. He spent most of her informative school years traveling and working long hours for the military. In fact, through most of her childhood he wasn't around and when he was, he was always busy working. Kyra understood that he was off saving the world, as her family called it, but just once she wished he paid more attention to their family rather than the world. His job did have some rewards and it paid the bills; but Kyra would have rather forgone the benefits just to be able to spend more time with her father as she grew up. Move after move, her family relocated. Virginia, Germany, Italy, France and South Dakota just to name a few. She learned and grew not just physically, but mentally. The years for her seamed to whiz by as she developed her own style in clothing. She wore jeans with an array of shirt styles that she picked up while traversing the world with her mother and father. There were always constant challenges to overcome and her heart would blaze with joy as she accomplished each one. Always knowing she had her parent's support and love along the way. She spoke bits and pieces of many languages, understood their cultures and made many friends along the way. To her friends she was loyal and enjoyed their company as they did hers; knowing all the time that Kyra would be moving again and leaving that life behind. Every move for her was heartbreaking and invigorating at the same time. She felt sad that she was leaving her home and friends, yet excited for her new home and friends she would make there.

Her mother always said, "If the military wanted you to have a family they would have issued it and unfortunately for me they didn't."

"Maybe I will write the President of the United States and ask him to issue families for active duty military members who want a family," Kyra said to herself, as her father left the kitchen. When her father had gone her mother walked into the cozy kitchen.

"Hi mom," Kyra said, greeting her mother warmly.

Her mother went to the cupboard, got a cup and poured her first cup of coffee for the day. Then she smiled tiredly at Kyra.

"Kyra," she said. "Your bus is going to be here soon. You better hurry or you'll be late!"

Kyra had hoped there would have been some private time to talk to her mother about the other night, but it seems she was on some sort of PMS trip.

"Yes Mom!" Kyra replied, politely.

She ran upstairs, grabbed her jacket and back-pack from the bedroom floor and stuffed her jacket into the largest pocket. Then she hurried out the door to the bus stop.

Hurray, she thought. *Here comes the bus.*

The bus that was filled with kids her age, kids that tormented her at school everyday. If her mother could only hear her thoughts, she would be appalled by the silent cynicism Kyra had for the many difficult events she had going on in her life, but she figured since her mother couldn't hear her, 'why not?' It couldn't hurt and it would help her to release some stress without hurting or bothering anyone else; as long as she kept burning the eternal hope that no bad will happen that she can't deal with.

"Oh look," Noelle said to her friend Shannon. "You were right. She has *LOSER* written all over her shirt."

She was giggling and pointing at Kyra as she climbed aboard the bus. Kyra's shirt had the capital letter L printed all over it; the design was a famous designer's label that her father had bought for her when he was in France. Following Noelle's lead all the other kids on the bus were a buzz about her shirt too.

"At least she's honest and knows she's a loser." Someone boasted, as she walked down the isle and sat in the first empty seat she could find.

It brought back memories of when she was five years old; her mother took her to a park on base near their home. Kyra wore her favorite outfit; torn jeans, a loose white t-shirt, with the Puddily Pops logo, and her favorite athletic shoes which were covered in lightening bolts that made her feel as if she could climb and run like the wind. When she was dressed in that outfit she felt invincible! She and her mother climbed, ran and laughed all day. While Kyra was chasing her mother around the playground, trying to catch her, an older girl pushed her hard from behind knocking her to the ground.

"Do you know your mother dresses you funny?" the girl said, sneering and pointing at Kyra's clothing. "I wouldn't be caught dead wearing an outfit like that."

Kyra stared at the girl like a deer caught in headlights. She couldn't understand why the girl was being so mean to her. In the distance she could hear her mother's voice asking her what was wrong. She hadn't realized her mother had come looking for her. Tears stained Kyra's cheeks. Her mother embraced her and she smiled. She felt safe snuggled in the warmth and comfort of her mother's arms.

While they walked home from the park, Kyra told her mother what the girl had said about her clothing.

"Do you like your clothes?" her mother asked.

"Yes, but…"

"Do you like who you are?"

"Yes…"

"Then be true to yourself. Like yourself, love yourself; embrace who you are and if you find you do not like yourself or what you have or are becoming or doing, change, but change because you want to."

Kyra's mother smiled and hugged her tightly in her arms. Even as a teenager, Kyra could still remember her mother's words, the way she smelled like lilacs, the softness of her hair as it brushed her cheek that day. Her mother seemed so wise to her, yet so fragile in a world were strong means to tell it like it is instead of the usual silent humility she practiced and taught. Kyra now high school age, with smooth shoulder length hair the color of cocoa with swirls of cinnamon and wide set steel blue eyes that snapped like clouds during a storm. She had a distinguished nose and chiseled cheeks that gave the impression she was a throwback to ancient roman times. Her body petite in stature at 5' 2" and around 105 pounds, she carried it with all the grace of an Olympian ready for competition. In her view, she was not beautiful, but not ugly either, while dressing to please her rather than the masses; however, that did not mean that she did not feel the pain of persecution.

"LOSER, LOSER, LOSER," another kid chanted, until the bus driver yelled at them to be quiet.

Kyra slouched down in her seat pretending to be studying. Quietly telling her self, it didn't matter what they said.

Kyra held back her tears; she was resolved not to cry, but the urge to cry won out and tears rolled down her rosy cheeks.

"Loser!" Noelle and Shannon yelled, as they got off the bus, ignoring what the bus driver had told them.

Kyra waited until all the other seats were vacant before she trudged off the bus and into the school.

The hallways were bustling. Lockers were slamming and the halls were alive with chatter as kids hurried off to their first class of the day. Kyra scanned the crowds searching for Aaron, hoping he would be waiting for her today as he was yesterday after school. When she did not see him, she searched the crowded halls for any familiar face that was at the beach last night. There were a few kids that might have looked familiar, but she wasn't sure, so she hurried off to class. After a string of classes, Kyra made her way to lunch, sat in her usual seat and studied the popular kids at their popular table and wondered what made them all the rage? The popular kids, she felt, often acted vulgar and intellectually arrogant, weren't as good-looking as they believed; however she did believe that there were exceptions where a few of the popular people acted just the opposite.

"Can I sit here?" a disembodied voice asked.

Kyra jumped in her seat and turned around quickly. Andrea was standing in front of her dressed in tight jeans, topped off by a blue sweater. She was holding a lunch tray in her hands and waiting patiently for an answer.

"Uhm—ya—go head. Good to see you again Andrea."

"Thanks," she said casually, and then she pulled out a chair and sat next to her.

Kyra watched her eat, not wanting to break the silence. She wasn't sure if she should talk to Andrea about that night.

"Would you like some of my dessert, Kyra?"

Kyra looked at the gooey brown mess on Andrea's plate, feeling a little awkward by her friendliness.

"No thanks. I'm full."

"Okay, your loss. Once it's gone it's gone." Andrea teased, filling her mouth until her lips were covered in the brown goo.

Feeling a somewhat brave by Andrea's seemingly relaxed friendship, Kyra thought it was time to ask a few questions.

"Andrea? What exactly happened last night?"

Andrea swallowed, wiped her mouth with the back of her hand and looked into Kyra's eyes.

"You were there. What do you think happened?"

Kyra smiled. She liked people who could think for themselves and rather than Andrea telling her forthright, she rephrased it back into a question. She leaned in closer to her, afraid others might hear her.

"I think you all changed into dragons."

Andrea grinned earring to earring; her dark wide set eyes sparkled in delight.

"If you know then why are you asking me?"

"So you really did turn into dragons!"

Andrea didn't refute what Kyra said and she didn't look at her like she was some kind of lunatic. Kyra closed her eyes in shear relief, absorbing the information, as if afraid it was going to dissipate and she would be the harebrained one. She was just about to ask Andrea how they did it when the bell rang; signaling lunch was over. By the time Kyra reopened her eyes to ask her question Andrea was gone.

"See ya!" Andrea called. She dumped the contents of her tray in the trashcan and made her way to her next class.

"Bye," Kyra chimed.

Just one-hour left until Biology and maybe some more answers, she thought.

When the final bell rang, Kyra was elated. She had to admit to herself that she had never been this excited about going to Biology class before Aaron stumbled into her life. She hurried to class, rounded a corner and clumsily crashed into Noelle's best friend, Shannon.

"Look Noelle, it's the loser," Shannon said. "Watch where you are going next time, loser."

"Sorry," Kyra offered.

She was flooded with relief when she saw Aaron, sitting in his black spoke racing like wheel chair, waiting for her outside the classroom.

"Aaron? You're here!" Kyra said, her heart was pounding so loud and fast she wondered if Aaron could hear it as well.

"Why wouldn't I be?"

"Well, you know, last night." She shrugged.

"Hey, it's not like it was a one night stand," he teased, grinning at her. "We better get settled before we're late for class."

"But what about last..."

She never got to finish what she was going to say because Aaron wheeled expertly around her and headed into the class. Kyra was a bit perturbed about his behavior and she wondered why he was being so evasive about the othert night. Aaron sat in the back of the room at a table that was low enough for his wheel chair. She, on the other hand, sat in the middle of the room precariously balanced upon a stool with her feet dangling in the air. The tables were made for a person of average height so an average person could work comfortably.

Neither Kyra nor Aaron was average by any means. Their teacher, Mr. Wilson, gave them a surprise quiz about the differences between viruses and bacteria. Lucky for Kyra she studied that section before going out the other night and she breezed through the quiz quickly. She turned to see how Aaron was doing on the quiz. He was finished with his too and passing the time reading a book. On the book's cover were dragons. Kyra found if she squinted, she could just make out the title: *Norse Mythology*.

When the bell rang, Kyra pushed her way through to the back of the class, offering apologies to students she bumped into while trying to reach Aaron. She reached Aaron's table, but to her surprise he was gone. She looked around the classroom, but he was nowhere in sight; she hung her head and the glint in her eyes was gone. She slowly left the room, extremely disappointed.

"Looking for me?" a voice beckoned to her.

She spun around quickly, startled and surprised; Aaron was sitting behind her, in his wheelchair, smiling brightly.

"I guess we had the same idea," he said. "I went to your table looking for you and I guess we missed each other."

Kyra felt her face flush with heat and in her mind she thought that maybe he wasn't being evasive after all.

"Aaron," Kyra said, trying to keep her composure. "I want to talk to you about last night."

"Same time, same place?" he said, ignoring her statement.

"No I want to talk now!" she demanded.

"We can't talk now. I have to get to class. But I'll leave you with a little riddle. When are your parents, not your parents and how much do you know about the Vikings landing in North America?"

"What kind of riddle is that?" she said, but before she could get an answer, Aaron sped off with a wave over his shoulder.

"See you tonight Kyra!"

But Kyra knew her mother wouldn't let her go out two nights in a row, especially on a school night. The time had come; it was now or never. She would set the stage to ask her mother about meeting Aaron again. She picked dinnertime because she knew her mom was usually easier to talk to when her stomach was full.

Later that night, as they ate dinner, Kyra told her mother about her adventures the night before.

"Mom," Kyra said to her mother while they ate. "I had a great time last night!"

"I'm glad to hear that honey," her mother replied.

"Mom?"

"Yes dear."

"Since I came home on time the other night and I had such a great time. Do you think I could meet Aaron again tonight? I really like him. And he's bringing some friends this time. You know I could really use some new friends."

"This boy really means that much to you?"

"Yes, he does."

Kyra sat back and waited for the usual lecture about how nice girls don't do this and nice girls don't do that. As well as, how girls who aren't so nice get into trouble. Her mother never said what kind of trouble not so nice girls got into, but Kyra thought she used the same lecture her mother gave her when she was a young girl.

She was sure her mother knew times had changed, but old habits died hard.

"Kyra, you can go under one condition."

Kyra stood, shifting from foot to foot, waiting for her terms.

"Take my cell phone again and call me when you get to Barkers Island."

Her mom stood up, reached out, and handed Kyra the cell phone.

"No problem mom. I can do that! Thanks!" she said, taking the cell phone in hand.

Quickly, she ran off to her room before her mother could come up with more terms.

How did she know I was going to Barkers Island? Kyra thought. *I didn't tell her where I was going.*

It was five thirty, according to the clock in her room. She still had some time before her date with Aaron, so she turned on her computer and logged onto the Internet. She wanted to search for information about when the Vikings first came to North America and if there were any myths or speculation written on the subject. Her search yielded information about Vikings landing in what is now known as Canada. They made a small settlement, stayed for a while and then left. She also found information about the mythology of trolls, dwarfs, the Norse Gods and a little about dragons. She found nothing that linked dragons, Vikings and North America or what the Vikings brought with them to North America. The lack of information was frustrating, so she clicked off her computer and made herself ready for whatever the night's activities would bring.

Chapter 5
A PLACE TO BELONG

"Aaron," Kyra asked when she had arrived at Barkers Island. "Where is everybody?"

Aaron was sitting alone in front of the whaleback ship. Kyra had completely forgotten to call her mother like she promised.

"You know how it is Kyra. They have their own things to do. Last night they came because they were curious about whom I was seeing. That's all."

She was alone at last, alone with a dragon. The boy with the caramel colored eyes lightly dipped in dark chocolate. The eyes she could no doubt get lost in.

"Kyra? Kyra!"

"Huh?" She answered, waking up from her daydream.

"Am I so boring that you have to day dream when you're with me?" he smirked, reached out and gently caressed her cheek.

"No! No. I was just thinking."

She never let on what the affect his eyes had on her. She was mesmerized by him.

"So Aaron," Kyra said, smiling. "What are we going to do tonight? Jump in the lake, cascade over mountains, or just talk?"

She was so busy staring into his dreamy eyes that he had already changed into his dragon form and flipped her onto his back.

"Aiii...!" Kyra screamed, from the sudden weightlessness she felt and landed straight onto his back.

Let's talk, she heard him say in her mind as they flew low over the water.

"Boat! Boat!" Was all she could scream, as a boat shot out into their path. Kyra closed her eyes and braced herself for impact. She felt the slight shift in Aaron's muscular body and he coasted effortlessly out of the boats way.

"You can open your eyes now," he gurgled and snorted.

Was he laughing! She thought.

"Ya go ahead and laugh at me," she fumed. "You wouldn't think it so funny if we would have crashed."

His gurgling and snorting continued. He was laughing so hard his body was shaking violently; it reminded Kyra of a small earthquake. His shaking was tickling her as she hung on for dear life, trying not to fall off.

"Stop... hahaha...that!" she laughed uncontrollably.

Your wish is my command, he thought into her mind.

They landed on top of the Aerial Lift Bridge.

It was a steel girder bridge overlooking Lake Superior and it was an ideal spot for viewing the area. The glow of the Duluth/Superior lights was all around them as they gazed at the pristine beauty of the lights, the lake and the night. The crisp air nipped at their noses while they watched small white shapes floating and the reflection of the city lights on the lake.

"Those are seagulls." Aaron said, pointing at the white shapes.

"*Seagulls*? I thought they would find some warm, dry place to sleep on land."

"Seagulls are opportunists. They sleep in their nests when they have young, otherwise they sleep anywhere; as long as there aren't any predators around, and I don't think Lake Superior has many predators that can eat a live healthy seagull."

"Do you eat seagulls?"

"Na, some of the others do, but for me they're too feathery. Last time I tried one it took me weeks to get the feathers out of my teeth! *Yuck!*"

I hope he brushes his teeth and to think I wanted to kiss that mouth, yuck! She thought,

She wondered if he ate bats. Carefully, he grabbed her and lifted her off his back, setting her down on one of the girders and then he morphed back into human form. The winds off the lake frightened Kyra as it tugged at her, threatening to knock her off the beam. She struggled to maintain her footing.

"Aaron!" she cried, as her feet swept out from under her; her arms pin wheeling trying to regain her balance as she tumbled off the beam.

I'm falling! Her mind screamed. *Help!*

A sharp pain cascaded down her arm and punched into her shoulder.

"Gotcha!" he said in her ear, as he settled down on the beam, with Kyra sitting in his lap. He wrapped his strong-arms tightly around her and her heart slowly returned to normal. They sat there in silence watching the stars glittering, the waves cresting gently on the water and the clouds misting by the moon. The two of them sat together, with her in his arms, as the sounds of the lake filled the air with a gentle rhythm that matched the beating of their hearts. The ships continued to cast their dark swaying shadows on the lake reflecting every now and again a rolling glimmer of light.

"Kyra, what did you want to ask me?" Aaron asked, his hot breath tickling her ear.

"Huh? Oh!" she said, as his voice seeped through the fog of her mind, bringing her back to reality. "I wanted to know why are there dragons here and why this area? In all the books I read, dragons exist everywhere but here!"

"Dragons like humans are everywhere. It's just that we choose to live hidden. If most humans knew we really did exist, they would try to put us in zoo's and dissect us; trying to find out whether we were more like lizards or snakes. Through history we have learned that humans kill what they are afraid of, even themselves."

She turned and *kissed* him on the cheek, hoping that maybe he might kiss her back; instead, he continued conversing.

"We would rather live in the form of dragons, but with humans living almost everywhere on earth, in order for us to survive, we have to live as humans in human form."

She started to think about what might happened if someone, anyone who was not willing to keep their secret, proved Aaron and his kind existed.

"Aaron, can you choose what you look like as a human?"

"No, we can only choose the age."

"Your age! How old are you. As a dragon, I mean?"

She had never thought about how long the legends said dragons could live. She just assumed he was her age even in dragon years.

"Hmm—about 225 years old, give or take a couple years."

"Two Hundred and twenty-five years old! What could you possibly want with me? I'm a bit young. Don't cha think?"

Aaron laughed, as he explained to her how dragon age was similar to a dog's age. That in approximation of dragon age he was about the same age as she and had as much to learn about the world as she did.

"Feel better?" he said, laughing and hugging her tighter.

"Yes much better. I was starting to think all I was to you was a plaything."

"Never! Are you hungry?"

"A little. Why are you?"

"Famished!"

"Umm—you don't eat people do you?"

"Only those that annoy me," he chuckled teasingly.

"Whew! What a relief."

Feeling playful, she leaned close to his ear and whispered, "I don't annoy you. Do I?"

Aaron grabbed her and threw her high up into the, brisk windy, moonlit night. She tried to scream, but it got lost in her throat. She felt the icy wind caress her body, stealing her breath away when she tried to scream again. Swirls of gray danced before her eyes as she was beginning to pass out. She could only watch through the gray mist as the ground rose rapidly to meet her.

Aaron what did I do? her mind screamed.

Her body wrenched up with pain as she was pulled away from the gravity that had held her and tossed back into the frigid air, like a plastic bag caught in a wind current. Then with a half twist she was floating upright and landed safely on Aaron's smooth dragon back. Kyra gasped for air; her body trembled from the cold and her death defying experience. She clung to Aaron, seething, laying face down; her heart was pounding into his back.

"I'm sorry," he said, apologetically. "I didn't mean to scare you. Let's go get something to eat."

"I'm not hungry," she said, sitting up and kicking him sharply in his side.

"I said I was sorry, what more do you want? I was just playing. Please, please believe me when I tell you I would have never let anything happen to you!"

"PLAYING! You call that playing?"

"I understand how you wouldn't think that was playing. Not being able to fly and all."

"You got that right mister!" she said, and then she gave him another sharp kick in his side for good measure.

She doubted that he even felt her kick him, with his thick scaly hematite color hide, but it did make her feel a little better. They circled Canal Park, looking for a safe place to land and found a secluded unoccupied area on the rocky shores of Canal Park close to the walkway of the lighthouse.

"Where to?" Kyra asked.

"Follow my lead," Aaron said, changing into human form.

He grabbed her hand and pulled her up to the main area by the museum and led the way. They only had to walk a little ways before arriving at a restaurant.

Aaron held the door for her and she walked inside. The walls of the restaurant were covered with eclectic images of marathons that had been held in the area as well as some other items reflecting the regions flavor.

"Have you ever eaten here Kyra?" He asked, as the waitress showed them to their seats.

"Ya, the food's yummy."

"Yummy?"

"Yes, yummy."

Aaron ordered a big steak with all the works and Kyra politely smiled and ordered the same thing. Aaron was surprised at how bold Kyra was being and it surprised her too.

Why not, she thought. *Didn't he throw me off the top of the Aerial Lift Bridge? A girl can really work up an appetite once the shock wears off from a near death experience.*

"I guess you're afraid this might be you*r* last meal?"

"What do people think when they see you in a wheelchair at school and then using your legs when your not?"

Aaron gazed at her before answering.

Such beautiful eyes, she thought with a deep sigh.

"I just make sure to avoid them. Usually after school I go to places they aren't—unless of course they can change into birds and fly."

"Why the wheel chair? If you don't need it?"

"Actually during the day, I really do need it."

Aaron explained to her how he had to be in a wheelchair at school; that he couldn't walk even if he tried. It had something to do with the sun and the moon. When the sun was out he couldn't walk, but when the moon was out then he was able to walk normally.

"Why? What do the sun and the moon have to do with it? Were you always like this? I don't understand."

She looked wearily around the room to see if anyone had taken an interest in their conversation. The other patrons were too busy conversing on their own to pay any attention to them.

"One question at a time Kyra. To answer question three, yes I was born like this and for your second question no. I don't know why the sun and moon has that affect on me, but I do know this, the effects are permanent."

He sighed, rubbing the side of his head, trying to stem the headache he felt coming on. Kyra sat patiently, her hands folded in her lap, waiting for him to continue.

"I'm not the only dragon that..." He squirmed a little as if he was about to reveal a deep dark secret.

"So, how about those Twins," Kyra chirped in an attempt to break the rising tension.

"Twins, aren't they baseball? This is football season," Aaron said, grimacing.

Kyra smacked herself softly on the head with the palm of her hand.

How could I forget it was football season? She thought. *I lived on the Wisconsin/Minnesota border. All the rivalry going on between the Packer and Viking fans was almost as interesting as the sport itself.*

Their chattering ebbed when the waitress brought their steaming plates of food. They immediately started shoveling piece after piece into their mouths as if they hadn't eaten for days. Their plates literally licked clean, mouths wiped and drinks consumed. Aaron checked the time.

"We have to hurry or you're going to be late!" he said.

He paid for their meal and left a sizable tip for the server.

I wonder where he keeps his money when he's a dragon and how does he keep popping up with clothes on, Kyra thought.

Aaron turned and grinned at her; looking deep into her steely gray eyes.

"I know what you're thinking Kyra. The money is real, but the clothes are just an illusion. Actually, I'm quite naked."

She couldn't help staring at his him and looking him up and down. The thought made her face glow bright pink.

I'll never look at him the same! She thought.

"Oh—I'm so sorry," She said, turning away and giggling.

She rushed out the restaurant and Aaron followed quickly behind her.

"Follow me," Kyra said.

The night air was filled with a globe frosty mist as they ran down the almost deserted street. Aaron ran passed their first landing site on the rocks just beneath the lighthouse walkway and clamored to the path that led to the gleaming solitary white and black lighthouse that rose above the lake.

"Why are we going there?" Kyra asked.

"There are people on the rocks," he panted, slowing his pace.

He grabbed Kyra firmly by the hand and pulled at her to quicken her pace. They had almost reached the lighthouse when with a quick flick of his wrist; Kyra flew high into the air and landed on his back. She didn't even realize Aaron had changed into his dragon form. She didn't even scream this time when he flung her into the air.

"How did you do that?"

The wind whipped her voice away, making it into a whisper.

"How did I do what?"

"Change into a dragon so quickly? Isn't it difficult?"

"It's more difficult for me to change into human form than it is my original form. Think about it?"

"I guess so," she replied.

"You know Kyra, it would be much easier to communicate if you just thought about what you want to say rather than voice it."

How do I do that?

You just did. As long as you direct your thoughts to me I can hear them.

Great, I hope you didn't hear all the thoughts I've been thinking. How embarrassing!

Ya, isn't it. Don't worry Kyra; I haven't heard all your thoughts, he teased.

They landed carefully in the alley behind her house and Aaron melted back into human form.

"Good night, Aaron. I had a great time."

Before she could turn to leave, he grabbed her gently, pulled her towards him, leaned forward and kissed her full on her lips. Their faces were warmed with a rosy glow and they gazed deeply into each other's eyes.

"Goodnight," Aaron crooned softly.

"Goodnight," she said, in a whisper, not really wanting to speak the words.

Kyra pulled away, breaking the trance and ran quickly into the house. She shut the kitchen door, turned around and suddenly felt a little sick to her stomach; her father was standing in the kitchen waiting for her.

"Kyra, I was worried about you," he said, concerned and a bit angry.

"I tried to call you on the cell phone for the last hour and couldn't reach you."

His eyes were dark and the corners of his mouth willingly accommodated gravity.

"Well young lady. I'm waiting for an explanation."

He stood there with his feet firmly planted, shoulders erect and hands on his hips waiting sternly for an answer. He was glaring at her as if she had committed a cardinal sin. She knew she was in seriously trouble.

"Hi Honey," her mother said. She walked into the kitchen and stood next to her husband. "Did you have a good time?"

She heard what her husband had said and before Kyra could answer she asked for the cell phone.

"Here you go mom," Kyra said, sheepishly. Then she awkwardly unclipped the cell phone from her belt and handed it to her mother.

They watched silently as Sunny flipped the phone open, holding it up in front of her husband and pointed to the screen. Then she whispered something in his ear. He shook his head in disbelief and wearily rubbed his hand down his face.

"My fault," Sunny said.

Kyra's father sighed tiredly.

"It's okay Kyra. Your mother has just informed me that she forgot to turn on the ringer before she gave you the phone. Next time you use her cell phone please check to make sure that it's on."

Kyra stood looking at her father in disbelief and at the same time she realized how lucky she was at that moment. If the ringer had been turned on she would have been grounded to her room for at least a week.

"Kyra," he continued, "I was just worried that something might have happened to you," and then he added, "I love you."

Kyra hadn't run to her father and hugged him in years, but that night was an exception.

"I love you too dad," she said, squeezing him as tightly as she could.

He had been so busy much of her life she had almost forgotten how worried he got when she wasn't safe at home. When Kyra was in sixth grade a friend who lived on a farm invited her by for her first sleep over. But before she even got to go her father had heard a news report on the television about a recent bear attack in that area.

He was so worried that a bear might break into the house that Kyra would be staying in that he forbade her to go. It wasn't until Kyra's mother reassured him that she would be safe and that the news report said that a bear, looking for food, had attacked some campers in their tents, who failed to secure their food properly. With some reluctance her father finally lifted the restriction and allowed her to go. It was then that she knew her father really loved her and that his love for her would never wane.

Kyra, off the hook in the meantime, dragged herself up the stairs to her room. She was dead tired from all the fresh air, food and flying as a passenger on Aaron's back. She was still puzzled by the riddles Aaron had told her earlier. On the bright side, she finally did get some of her questions answered; only now she had even more questions. She undressed, took a quick shower, slid into her pajamas and climbed into her soft, comfy, twin size bed. She could hear her mother's light padded footsteps crossing the room.

"Goodnight Kyra," her mom said tenderly. She pulled the quilt up around her neck and rested them just under her chin. She leaned over and planted a gentle kiss on Kyra's forehead.

"I love you," she whispered.

"Good night mom," Kyra garbled as she drifted off to sleep.

It was still dark when she awoke; her heart was throbbing erratically in her chest. She jumped gracefully to her feet—ready to protect herself from the threat she felt; she was shivering and wet from perspiration. Glancing defensively around the room, she didn't notice anything out of the ordinary. That was until she became aware of a blurred reddish brown smudge on the glass outside her window; it looked like some weird handprint. When her eyes had adjusted to the dim moonlight shining in her room, she could see that the smudge was indeed a handprint—it was a hand-claw similar to Aaron's.

"Aaron!" her mind screamed out his name. It was all she remembered when she woke, drenched in sweat, lying on the carpeted floor; the sun was peeking at her through the window and the print that she thought was a smudge in her dreams was real.

Chapter 6
THE CODE

"Nothing, but a little late fall house cleaning," Kyra said to her mother when she was asked what she was doing. Sunny stood in the doorway watching her daughter clean. The windows of their house tilted in for cleaning so that made it easy for Kyra otherwise she would be frantic about how she was going to hide the bloody print sticking solidly to the middle of the glass pane. She wiped the last of the window cleaner off the window and she could only wonder if Aaron was playing some sort of prank on her. She wondered if he had gotten injured somehow, or if one of the other dragons were trying to frighten her. She dismissed the thought immediately from her mind, but the question of how the bloody print got there still remained.

"Kyra," her mom said, before she left the room. "I know I usually fuss at you to clean your room, but it's forty degrees outside this morning and I don't think now is a good time to clean windows."

Kyra knew she was right. It was getting chilly in her room from having her window tilted open, but she was sure her mom would have freaked out if she had left the window the way it was. Kyra got dressed quickly and ran down the creaking stairs to the kitchen; her mother was at her usual spot at the table, nursing a cup of coffee in hand and her father nowhere in sight.

"Where's dad?" Kyra asked, sitting at the table and pouring a bowl of cereal.

Sunny looked up from the book she had been reading, her brows knitted together.

"Did you forget he had to go to work this morning?"

Now she had done it. She made her mother's radar go off by asking her a question she herself should have known.

Nervously Kyra sloshed the milk all over the counter top.

"Oops! I'll clean it up," she said.

She reached for a paper towel, ripping it off the rack and laying it on top of the spill, letting the towel do most the work.

"Hey mom, these paper towels really do absorb a lot!" she said smiling. She picked up the sopping towel and threw it away.

"What's wrong with you today Kyra?" her mother asked suspiciously. "First you're up early this morning cleaning the windows then you forget your father had to work today. It's not like you. What's wrong?"

Kyra wanted to tell her mom about everything. About Aaron and his friends being dragons and about the bloody claw print, but she was afraid.

She was afraid that her mother would never believe her and would probably be grounded for life. So she did the next best thing. She shrugged her shoulders, shoved a spoonful of cereal into her mouth and mumbled, "I don't know."

It was a safe response that most children learn, as soon as they can talk, to defend themselves from things they do not want to answer. Kyra felt guilty as she watched her mother silently get up and pour herself another cup of coffee. Her mother, like some adults, never forgot what it was like to be an adolescent; she knew exactly what Kyra was doing. Kyra glance over at the book her mother had been reading and the title made her eyes widen. *Norse Mythology* was the title of the book; it was the same book she had seen Aaron reading in school.

"Mom! Where did you get that book?"

Startled by the urgency in Kyra's voice her mom turned quickly, knocking her cup off the counter and sending it crashing onto the floor.

"Calm down," her mom said, as she stooped to clean up the mess. "I found it in your backpack. I'm sorry if I upset you. I didn't think you'd mind."

"Oh, no mom," Kyra said. She picked up the book and shoved it roughly into her backpack. "I don't mind. I just forgot I had that book, that's all."

Kyra glanced cautiously at her mother to see if she believed her and it seem as though she did. It made her stomach churn to think that she had to lie to her.

"Oh," her mom said gingerly. "This fell out of your book." She was holding a tattered piece of paper, folded into a square. "In case you're wondering," she continued, "I didn't open it. I respect your privacy."

The morning was turning out to be one of those days when Kyra wished she had stayed in bed. Filled with guilt of the lie she had told and her mother's declaration of how she respected her privacy, she did the only thing she could do. She smiled an uttered, "Thanks mom." Then she blindly stuffed the note in her back pocket, kissed her mother on the cheek, grabbed her coat and headed out the door. Kyra's mind focused on the sidewalk in front of her as she quickly walked to the bus stop.

She arrived at school on time and scanned the hallways between classes, hoping to catch a glimpse of Aaron, Andrea or of any of the other dragons she had seen that first night at Barkers Island. As the day rolled on she hadn't seen any of them, but she was hopeful that at lunch perhaps Andrea would be there. Her mind was consumed with theories about the bloody claw print and she hoped that maybe Andrea might have some theories of her own. Perhaps it wasn't blood at all, but red clay. Or maybe it was just a prank one of the other dragons had played to frighten her. Though her theories were plausible, two most likely reasons played in her mind. It was either a prank or perhaps it was some sort of warning. If only she could find Aaron or Andrea they might be able to tell her. Lunchtime came and she decided to buy lunch. She grabbed an apple, a salad and a bottle of water. Then she proceeded to the cashier.

"Two dollars and twenty cent," the cashier said.

Kyra reached into her back pocket and pulled out two dollar bills. The note her mother had given her had fallen out of her pocket and onto the floor. Hanging onto the bills she fished in her front pocket for twenty cents and found two dimes.

She dropped the money into the cashier's hand, picked the note up from the floor, snatched up the tray and looked for a private table. She found the perfect table. It was close enough to the cafeteria doors so if Andrea should come in she wouldn't miss her. Kyra opened the paper, being careful not to tear it, and spread the note out on the table. The note was comprised of strange symbols that looked something like hieroglyphics.

[symbols]

I know I've seen symbols like this somewhere, she thought, *but where. Maybe in history class when we they were studying ancient Egypt.*

"Hey," a student said to his pal as they walked passed her to the lunch line, disrupting her thoughts. "I heard they're serving wing dings today!"

She sat through lunch, carefully studying the note and trying to decipher it; sneaking in bites of her apple in between. Her salad, laid forgotten, turned limp on the tray. Bringgg—the bell rung; it was time for her to move on to her next class. Kyra got up for the table, jammed the note deep into her backpack and stuffed the leftover lunch in the trash. She was hopeful that Aaron would be in Biology to ease her fears and explain what was going on. On the way to class her head started throbbing. At first it was a dull pain just behind her ear, then it steadily increase as she made her way to class.

"Stress headache," she muttered, trying to comfort herself, as the pain in her head amplified two fold.

"Kyra. Kyra," she heard someone behind her whisper.

She turned to see who it was, but all she saw were a sea of faces bobbing to their next class.

I must be hearing things, she thought.

Until she heard her name whispered again only this time more urgent.

"What!" she replied, frustrated.

She twirled around abruptly and smacked into Mr. Wilson; the biology teacher, and almost knocked him off his feet. Shocked by the incident, he could only sputter and shake his head as sweat bead from his brow. Kyra offered him a quick apology and scooted off to her next class hoping the time would go by quickly. As she sat in class waiting for it to be over, the thrumming in her head worsened; she started to shiver and sweat poured down her face.

"Just a little bit longer," she coaxed herself, wiping the sweat with her sleeve, trying desperately to hold out until the class was over. She wanted to ask the teacher for a pass to go to the nurse's office, but she was afraid that she might miss Aaron.

"KYRA!" a voice screamed in her head.

She started trembling uncontrollably; sweat poured from her like a sprinkler and an intense pain tore her head in two. Her body plummeted off her chair down to the cold tiled floor and she landed with a sickening thump. Kyra never heard the bell ring for biology.

"Ky—ra," a ghostly voice whispered in the night; the moon was lighting up everything around her in an ethereal blush; she saw waves undulating far below her, embracing the rocks that jutted maliciously out of the water.

It was reaching for her, calling out her name. Kyra teetered on the edge of the cliff, imploring her body not to reply. She could only watch, feeling the alarm rise up in her as her arms reached out to them.

"Ky—ra," they called, "come to us."

She wobbled, resisting, as her feet started moving closer to the edge. Amongst the waves, sitting on the largest rock she could see a gloomy figure, battered and bloody looking up at her with big dark sad eyes.

"Ky—ra," it called up at her, "RUN!"

The dark silhouette's command shocked her out of her stupor. She regained control over her body and mind; she spun around and ran howling.

"Noooo...!"

Then she realized the broken figure on the rocks had been Aaron.

Kyra found herself running through the woods, branches slashing and grabbing at her as if trying to stop her. When she could run no more, she tumbled to the ground and sobbed. She wept for Aaron, wondering if he was still alive or if the crashing tide washed him away. She cried for herself; lost, afraid, and confused. Wondering how she had got to the cliff when her last memory was of her sitting safe in her classroom at school, waiting for the bell to ring for her biology class. The only class she was able to see Aaron in; the only one who might hold the answers that she sought. A shadow flickered across the ground. Looking up Kyra saw a large dark shape looming just above the trees, directly over her head. She crouched lower, burying her head into her shaking arms, trying to shield herself from the shadows view.

"Ky—ra," it sang to her. Its words vibrated through her mind. "Don't be afraid."

She heard the rustling of branches as it made its descent. She looked up and was startled to see Andrea looming protectively over her. Andrea was more beautiful than she remembered; the moonlight shimmered in waves off her dark lavender scales and the shape of her dragon frame was sleek and powerful. Kyra wanted to tell her about Aaron and ask her what was happening. Andrea gently picked her up and placed Kyra carefully on her back.

"Hang on," Andrea said, her voice soft as a lullaby. "I'm here to bring you home."

Chapter 7
THE AWAKEN

"Kyra, are you awake?" a soft motherly voice asked, hovering just beyond her touch. She reached out to the gentle voice, struggling to embrace it.

"Kyra," the familiar voice called a little closer.

"*I'm coming,*" Kyra called to the warm voice, scrambling to connect with it before it could fade away.

Her eyelids felt as heavy as an overstuffed backpack on the night before exams as she tried in vain to raise them.

"Oh Kyra, we're here," her mother said. Kyra recognized the sound of her mother's voice as she whispered in Kyra's ear. "We're here honey."

She fought harder to open her eyes, with gravity fighting just as hard to keep them sealed. Slowly a string of light appeared to her, beckoning her to follow its path and as she did her parents weary faces came into view. Kyra tried to speak to them, but her tongue felt thick and dry.

"Here honey, drink this," her father said.

He gently maneuvered the straw in a cup he was holding and placed it in her mouth. Kyra never thought water could taste so good, as she sucked it in greedily.

"Not too much now," he said softly, just before he pulled the drink away.

She glanced around at her surroundings unsure of where she was; she saw that the room was colored in a generic salmon pink, while mauve paisley print curtains were pulled off to the side revealing the bright sunshine that lay behind them; it was daytime. She assumed by the setting and colors of the room as well as the adjustable cold metal clad bed that she was in the hospital. She remembered feeling fuzzy as if her head was going to explode; the weightless feeling of falling, then the thick darkness taking over and surrounding her in a blacken tomb. Then poof, as if by magic, she was standing on a cliff at Split Rock Lighthouse, gazing through the darkness down at the rocks below. Aaron was calling to her from below and telling her to run. She remembered running through the woods lost and confused and Andrea had come to her aid in her dragon form and brought her back home. But she wasn't home. She was in the hospital. It was as if she was dreaming, but it was all too real to be a dream.

"What happened to me?" she asked, barely recognizing the sound of her own voice.

Both her parents were standing by her bed, with deep dark bags under their eyes, glancing worriedly at her and smiling nervously.

"You don't remember?" her parents chimed in unison.

Kyra shook her head slowly side to side, then took a deep breath and began her tale of what she did remember. Feeling secure and brave with both her parents there, she included the parts about the cliff and the dragons. By the time she was done, her parents hugged her tightly, one on each side, and assured her that there was no such things as dragons. That she had been laying in the hospital unconscious for a week, not standing on some cliff.

"I've been here a week?" Kyra asked.

Her mother gently caressed her brow, while her father told her about the weeks events since she been in the hospital. Kyra fell asleep listening to her father's strong soothing voice and feeling her mother's relaxing touch.

When Kyra opened her eyes again, it was dark outside and her parents were gone. She glanced around her room and noticed the clock read 10:18 pm. Kyra had never been in a hospital except for when she was born; she wasn't sure what she was supposed to do. She wondered if the hospital served meals at that time of night and wished her parents were there, they would know what to do. She could feel her stomach rumbling; it was telling her it wanted food.

"Nurse, anyone, I am awake now and very hungry. Could I please get something to eat?" She called out towards the door and waited quietly for a response, but none came.

"Hello!" she called again. "Nurse! Anybody! I'm awake now and very hungry!"

She heard brisk footsteps outside in the hallway, but they went pass her door and faded away further down the hall. She tried to sit up to no avail. The more she tried the dizzier she became. Eventually she finally made it to sitting position, the dizziness faded and a dull pain thrummed inside her head. Getting out of bed, she realized, was going to be much more difficult than what she originally thought. Her bed had a railing that blocked her from scooting off the side. She pushed, pulled and tried to slide it out of the way, but couldn't; it was at that point she got the bright idea to go over the railing. Kyra turned over on her hands and knees so she could lift one leg over it at a time. As soon as she got the first leg over, she lost her balance and fell to the floor landing solidly on her backside. She quickly found out that hospital floors were not padded. She carefully got to her feet, steadied herself and shuffle towards the door. She didn't get very far when she felt something pull sharply on her hand, sending a mild jolt of pain to the pulled area. The pulling she felt was a long clear tube attached to some sort of bag and the other end of the tube was attached to her hand with tape. She tried to jerk her hand away, but it hurt worse the second time; her heart was beating erratically in her chest and beads of sweat rolled off her forehead. She couldn't move forward and she wasn't sure she would be able to climb back over the bars onto the bed.

"HELP!" she yelled, trying to make sure someone, anyone heard her.

"They can't hear you," the voice of a female said calmly behind her.

Kyra jumped back startled and almost ripped the I.V out in the process. She cried out in pain and fright when she felt strong arms picking her up and placing her back on her bed. She relaxed when she recognized the long silky hair that hid her visitors face from view.

"Andrea, what are you doing here?"

Andrea smiled like the cat that swallowed the canary. Then she started to pace back and forth in front of Kyra's bed before turning to look out the window. Kyra could see her reflection in the window pane; her smile had vanished and was replaced by sadness and concern.

"Did you find the note that Aaron left for you?" she asked, sullenly.

"What note?" Kyra replied. "He never gave me a note?"

Suddenly she remembered and started looking frantically around the room for her backpack.

"Andrea," Kyra said excitedly. "The note I think you're talking about was in my backpack, but I don't know what happened to it after I passed out."

Andrea's reflection in the window frowned a little more.

"Maybe it's somewhere in the room. There's a closet by the door we could look in."

Andrea turned around and looked at Kyra; then she held up her hand in a gesture for her to stay in bed while she checked the closet.

"Its empty." she whispered sadly.

Then she closed the door and walked over to Kyra's bed. She plopped herself down on the end of the bed and explained.

"When I woke, the same morning you were taken ill, I saw a bloody handprint on the window. I went to school that morning, but I didn't see Aaron all day.

I did, however, hear his voice calling out my name. Last night I had a dream that you were lost in the woods, by Split Rock Lighthouse, and couldn't find your way out. In the dream I rescued you and delivered you safely home."

Andrea paused and Kyra stared at her like she had seen a ghost.

"I had the same dream," Kyra said.

And then she went on to tell Andrea about the handprint on the window, the voice she heard in the hallway at school and the sudden explosion in her head. Andrea cried when Kyra told her that in that same dream she saw Aaron on the rocks, calling to her to run.

"What's going on?" Kyra asked, hoping for an answer.

Andrea only shook her head sadly.

"I don't know, but I do know none of this is good. I had hoped the note Aaron gave you would tell me."

Andrea told Kyra that most of the dragons that lived there were either too young or didn't care to learn the history of their kind in North America. Aaron was the exception. Aaron loved studying history of all kinds and when he was younger he had gone off with the old ones, for a few years, to learn about their history. The dragon elders taught Aaron everything about dragon history and entrusted him to keep dragon folk law alive. It was then she remembered something Aaron said about a note. A note that he needed to give to Kyra because he felt she was *the one*. Before Kyra could ask her what *the one* was, Andrea looked gently into her stormy eyes and explained in a whisper that they believed *the one* to be a human with a dragon's heart.

"I'm all-human," Kyra said, anxiously. "A dragon's heart wouldn't fit in my body!"

"Relax Kyra. What it means is a human that has a connection to a dragon's soul."

"Dragons have souls?"

Kyra could see the shift in Andrea's face and knew that her question angered her. Andrea's eyes flashed and her face reflected her dragon side.

"Why wouldn't we have souls? Don't all creatures have souls, or do you think they are just for humans!"

Kyra's face flushed crimson and she gazed down at the sheets on her bed.

"I'm sorry Andrea," Kyra said, apologetically. "I wasn't thinking when I said that."

But when she lifted her head, Andrea was gone. Kyra lay in her hospital bed blinking back tears and thinking about all that had transpired in the last two weeks. Somehow a part of her always knew that dragons existed in Superior, Wisconsin. She knew it even as a young child. Once a year, when she visited her Grammy in the fall, they would gaze into the clear northern night sky looking at the stars above. There were times, during their star gazing, they both noticed winged silhouettes gliding in the sky. Kyra's Grammy told her they were seagulls, but Kyra knew they were something else. Seagulls didn't have long tails and rarely flew in the pale moonlight. One crisp cold rainy night, when Kyra found it hard to sleep, her Grammy rocked her in her arms and told her a story about dragons. At first Kyra was surprised that her Grammy had known any stories about dragons, but as her Grammy started speaking, Kyra became so enthralled by the tale she almost felt she had been there.

The dragons were hunted mercilessly from the earliest time that humans and dragons inhabited the earth.

The dragons killed humans as if they were playthings and the humans killed dragons to prove their valor. Each in their own right had their reasons for hunting each other toward extinction. In the end, the dragons almost became extinct. While the humans seemed to thrive, reproducing at four times the rate than dragons could and becoming adults much sooner. The king of the European dragons was a wise king and saw the tide of their existence turning. No longer were dragons the top predators but humans as they gained in knowledge and quantities. In a small Norse village lived a family whose lives intertwined by fate to the dragons as well as the dragons to them, they called this family The One.

The Dragon king went to them for help, asking if they would take a treacherous secret voyage to find a safe haven for their last clutch of dragon eggs and a few dragons that would watch over the eggs and them across the seas. The Ones agreed, loading their boat with provisions and dragon eggs, set out across previously uncharted seas to find a safe haven for their dragon kin. They sailed for months across the ocean guided by the changing stars, stopping on land every now and then to rest, hunt and repair their boat. When they were exhausted and near starvation the dragons that followed chortled and helped guide the boat into a safe harbor.

The land was lush and green. Filled with birds and other animals the dragons could hunt for food. There were cliffs by the sea that offered a secure place for the dragon eggs to be stored until they were ready to hatch. Their job accomplished, they said goodbye to their dragon brethren before departing to sail back to their homeland, leaving the dragons to live in peace. In what is now believed to be the continent of North America.

Once home The Ones rarely spoke of the event because if anyone had found out what they had done it would have been sure death. So whenever they spoke about the dragons and the secret voyage, they told it as a folk tale to entertain little ones. As time went on The Ones were forgotten but the story lived, told from one generation to generation live on. Each believing that it was just a story, but in life, anything was possible, so you decide. Is the story real or an old folk tale?

It wasn't until her Grammy had told her that story that she realized what she had seen wasn't seagulls, but dragons! As Kyra became older, she methodically convinced herself through logic that it must have been her imagination, but now she had found out the truth; it was real all the time.

Kyra hadn't meant to fall back to sleep and the hunger that had gnawed at her stomach earlier still screamed for food.

Chapter 8
THE DETECTIVES

Kyra, once again, found herself at the cliff at Split Rock Lighthouse, standing precariously on the edge, the waves crashing on the rocks below, only this time she was screaming for Aaron to save her. She awoke startled out of her sleep by the dream as the bright morning sunlight shined through the window. She was still safe in the hospital for now from whatever her dreams were trying to communicate to her. Kyra was sitting up eating breakfast when her mom came in her hospital room and told her the doctor said she could go home. It wasn't long until a nurse came in smiling and removed the I.V. from her bruised hand.

Kyra quickly climbed out of the bed, grabbed the clothes her mom had brought for her, showered and got dressed; avoiding her mother's frazzled face. She was dressed and ready to walk out of her room when the nurse came in pushing a wheelchair and ordered her to climb in for a short ride. Staring at the big bright wheelchair, Kyra hesitated as if not sure she wanted a ride. The nurse quickly smiled and said, "Hospital policy," in a warm even voice, gesturing at the wheelchair.

"I'll go get the car," her mom said, pecking Kyra on the cheek.

The ride in the wheelchair to the hospital entrance seemed like it took forever. The nurse chattered about what a scare, Kyra gave them all and how glad she was to see that Kyra seemed to make a full recovery. Kyra nodded her head only half listening, barely acknowledging her comments as she organized in her mind the first things she needed to do when she got home.

When they pulled into their concrete driveway, Kyra opened the car door and jumped out; leaving her mom behind to bring in her personal effects. She wanted to hurry into the house and call Andrea, but the door was locked. Kyra smirked; she looked around to see if her mother had noticed, but she was busy pulling some packages out the trunk of the car. When her mother glanced up and saw her waiting, she hurried to the door, apologizing for keeping her waiting, and unlocked it. Kyra wasn't listening; she was focused on getting inside and as soon as the door swung opened, she rushed inside, ran up the stairs and went into her bedroom. She shut the door quickly behind her and noticed, out of the corner of her eye, a shadowy figure.

The shadow, she realized, was a person who had been standing behind the door. Kyra spun on her heels and stifled a scream deep in her throat. The unexpected intruder she quickly realized was Andrea.

"Andrea, you scared me!" Kyra said, panting.

Andrea looked scared and sad; Kyra walked over to her and hugged her tightly.

"I'm sorry about the other night," Kyra said. "The way I acted and…I'm scared too."

They sat on Kyra's bed and Andrea told her that more dragons had mysteriously disappeared.

"I had been with them when something huge dropped out of the sky; it grabbed hold of a couple of them and then it quickly wrenched them away. I listened, hoping they would call out, but the only sound I heard was the wind careening through the trees."

Andrea stared at Kyra, her dark, sparkling eyes were full with pain and confusion; dark shadows had taken residence under them. Kyra turned away, not wanting to look into Andrea's dull lifeless eyes, or the pain they held for the disappearance of Aaron and her friends. Kyra looked around the room; her eyes paused and settled on her backpack lying on the floor by her bed.

"The backpack," she said out loud. "The note should be in my backpack where I left it!"

She jumped off the bed in excitement, snatched up the backpack, zipped it opened and triumphantly pulled out the crinkled note.

"Whoopee! I found it!" she yelled, waving the note the in air for Andrea to see before thrusting it towards her face.

Andrea's face softened a bit and her eyes sparked with hope. Kyra smiled and handed her the note.

"Andrea," she asked, in a mild tone. "Can you read this?"

Andrea took the note and smirked.

"I'll try my best," she said.

Andrea gingerly opened the note and tilted her head side to side; her mouth was slightly open and her brow pursed, as she tried to decipher the strange looking writing. She gasped and then she grinned broadly and uttered one word, *"Wingdings."*

Kyra reached over and patted her shoulder comfortingly.

Andrea finally lost her mind, she thought. *How could she think of food at a time like this? Oh Andrea, I'm so sorry.*

What are you jabbering about?

You can hear my thoughts?

Yes. Your directing them at me, aren't you?

Well ya, I guess so. I didn't mean to. Are you like, all right?

Yes, I am! Aaron wrote the note in wingdings!

Wingdings? Is that like some kind of food you dragons like to eat?

No, wingdings are a type of encrypted font that's like on the computer.

Kyra was still bewildered; she stared at Andrea, holding back the urge to check her for fever. Andrea grabbed Kyra's hand, pulled her off the bed and dragged her over to the computer.

"Turn it on," she demanded.

Kyra stood there with a blank expression, alternating glances from the computer screen and then back to Andrea.

"Turn it on now!" Andrea commanded. "And go to your word program fonts."

Kyra's mind was starting to work overtime; she turned on the computer and waited for the start menu to pop up. Then she clicked with the mouse to the word program and pulled down the font menu.

"Wingdings," Andrea said, pointing at the computer screen.

"Oh, wingdings!" Kyra reiterated, smiling.

The two of them spent the next few minutes typing out each letter of the alphabet until they had every symbol on the note deciphered and then they wrote the letters under each symbol. They discovered, to their surprise that the note was a poem that read:

Banished dragons in the night
Causing lots of human fright
Chomp one, chomp two, chomp three, chomp four
Until they're knocking at your door
Head them off anyway you can
So they cannot bother man.

The poem sounded like something found in a children's nursery rhyme. Kyra looked up at Andrea; her face was dreamy and deep in thought. Then a tear trickled down Andrea's flushed cheeks.

"Andrea, what's wrong?" Kyra asked. "What is this all about? Banished dragons in the night. What was Aaron trying to say?"

Andrea nodded her head numbly as if someone had just told her that her dog was hit by a bus. Kyra reached over and grabbed a box of tissues from the nightstand.

"Here," she said, handing the whole box to Andrea. "You need these more than I do."

Andrea took a tissue from the box and wiped the tears streaming down her cheeks.

Her eyes, once and again, cast a quick glance at the note as if it was going to jump up and bite her at any given moment.

"This is an old dragon nursery rhyme," Andrea said, finally breaking her silence. "We all learned it as small nurslings."

Andrea's shoulders were slumped and her body swayed back and forth. Kyra leaned forward and embraced her warmly.

"It's going to be ok Andrea," Kyra cooed in her ear. "But why would Aaron code the nursery rhyme, if that is all it is?"

Kyra wanted to ask her why she was so upset, but she knew the answer was coming and she wasn't sure if she really wanted to hear it.

"Because," Andrea said, solemnly. "It's a nursery rhyme with a sinister meaning. Just like your Ring around the Rosy; it's one that has some truth in it."

Kyra remembered the rhyme well; she had been surprised to learn that a rhyme she had enjoyed as a child held something more sinister behind it; Ring around the Rosy was a rhyme associated with the plague that invaded Europe.

"What does it mean?" Kyra wanted to know.

Andrea sighed deeply, brought her legs up on the bed and hugged her knees tightly as if it would protect her from what she knew.

"When the dragons emigrated from Europe to North America," she said, mildly. "They created *the pact of three*. Firstly, they would never eat humans again. Secondly, they would live in human form, when they were among humans; the only exceptions would be *the ones*. Thirdly, the dragons would try to abide by human ways and laws in order to survive in peace. This included your economic system as it developed from something primitive to the way it is now.

Most dragons agreed, but a few older and bold younger ones would not abide by *the pact of three*. So, the council banished them into the farthest reaches of the north where humans usually did not or could not reside for very long."

Andrea paused and glanced over Kyra's shoulder at the window.

"Go on," Kyra said, anxiously.

"Well, before the dragons could be banished, they went on a rampage; killing and devouring as many humans as they could find before they were driven away. Fortunately for the humans there weren't many dragons around at the time. Anyways, about fifty years ago some very young dragons, I think could be considered preschoolers in human age, decided to play a joke on a leisure boat out fishing. The young dragon's swarmed around the boat in a circle and then they would leap over it to the other side and gurgle with laughter. The crew members on the boat were terrified. They panicked and a few of them hid below deck, but others grabbed fishing poles with hooks and any thing else they could find to chase away what they thought were sea serpents."

She paused enclosed her face with her hands and sobbed. Kyra pulled Andrea into her; wrapped her arms around her and gently rocked back and forth in an attempt to comfort her. Andrea quickly composed herself and began once again.

"There was a young dragon among the group that day named Matthew," she murmured under her breath. "He was killed by one of the fishermen brandishing a pole; it was skewered through his eye and into his brain. He died quickly. He was so very young and beautiful and he had everything to live for. But now he's dead."

Andrea sobbed like her heart had been broken and as far as Kyra was concerned it was. She held her friend even tighter, trying desperately to comfort her.

"Andrea," Kyra said softly. "You don't have to continue now. You can tell me later when you're feeling better."

Andrea shook her head no; she had to tell Kyra the rest because she feared that there might not be another chance.

"An older, pewter colored dragon saw what had happened to Matthew," her voice cracked as she began again. "Out of hurt and rage the pewter dragon swooped down from the sky, knocked the fishermen over the side of the boat and drowned him. Then he ate the man in two bites. The council reprimanded the young dragons for their actions and they banished the pewter dragon to the far north for his role. The young dragon that died that day was my brother and the pewter dragon, whose name was Günter, was my father."

"Oh Andrea," Kyra offered. "I'm so sorry."

"Wait, I'm not finished," Andrea said. "You have to hear the whole thing to understand." She composed herself took a deep breath and exhaled. "Aaron's grandfather, Jacob, tried to protect my father by defending his actions as instinctual. He argued that my father had done what any father would have done; avenge his own. But the council considered, Jacob's, defense of my father a blatant disregard for the pact and he too was banished."

Andrea turned and hugged Kyra; tears rolled from her eyes.

"I'm so sorry about your brother and father."

"Kyra," Andrea whispered softly. "It's okay. It was a long time ago. I hardly even cry about it anymore."

They both wiped the tears from their cheeks and laughed when they saw their reflections in the mirror.

"Andrea," Kyra asked a bit bewildered. "What does all this have to do with the nursery rhyme?"

Andrea stood up straight and glared at Kyra; her face was serious and her eyes were radiating.

"The banished dragons are back," she said with malice. "They're looking to claim what they feel is their rightful place in the world. They intend to use humans like you use cattle. Not a pretty picture huh?"

'No. It's not."

"Now that I know what's happening, I have to tell the others. I'll be back later and I think it is time you met my mother, especially since we are going to be spending a lot of time together."

Andrea grabbed Kyra and hugged her roughly. She was starting to become the sister Kyra never had.

"Andrea. How old are you anyways?"

She stepped back towards the door, her eyes twinkling.

"Much older than Aaron, wouldn't you say?"

Kyra couldn't help stifling a chuckle and she let loose with laughter.

"You must be a slow learner to be in high school at your age," she said giggling.

"Very slow," Andrea replied, and giggled too.

She pushed her dark hair out her face, walked through the door, down the stairs and out of the house. Kyra watched from her window as Andrea sauntered down the road like she didn't have a care in the world. Andrea stopped when she was confronted by an older man standing in her path. When she realized who it was she spun and ran back towards the house. Kyra gasped when she saw Andrea quickly mutate into a dragon, in broad daylight, and fly off into the sky.

Kyra looked back and the man that had frightened Andrea was still standing there grinning. Right before her eyes, he morphed into an iridescent white dragon; almost as white as the color of the clouds overhead. His teeth glistened and his claws were long and sharp. He leaped into the air and flew off in the same direction as Andrea.

I need to warn her! Kyra yelled in her mind. She was directing her thoughts at Andrea, hoping it would work for her as it did early.

Andrea! He's coming! Fly!

Kyra's heart nearly jumped out of her chest when the white cloudlike dragons face appeared at her window. He sneered at her; blood oozing from his mouth. The only thing separating them was a thin pane of glass. He tapped his gleaming razor sharp claw against the glass and she shrieked like a banshee. Kyra's mother burst into her room and pulled her away from the window. She held Kyra in her arm and asked her what had happened. Kyra's howls reverberated off the walls of the room.

"It's all right Kyra, mama's here," her mother whispered, over and over, rocking Kyra in her arms, until her screams ceased and she was calm.

Kyra stared at the window transfixed; she was expecting the white dragon to break through the glass and eat her in one bite. She took a deep breath and collected herself; she didn't want to worry her mother.

"It's nothing mom," she said softly. "I just thought I saw something."

"What?"

Kyra looked into her mother's worried eyes and grinned as if it was all some kind of bad joke.

Maybe she saw the dragon at my window when she came in. Kyra thought.

Kyra glanced back out the window; there was nothing there, but the bright blue sky and wispy clouds. She turned and looked at her mother's face and noticed how weary she looked.

"Kyra, why don't you rest for a little while? Her mother said. "You look very tired."

"Only if you do," Kyra replied. "But first I need to get something to drink."

Before her mother could respond, she quickly walked out of the bedroom, down the stairs and into the kitchen; she pulled the blinds over the kitchen window incase old cloudy decided to pay her another visit.

Better safe than sorry, she thought.

She did not want to see anything scarier than an ant the size of a crumb. She went into the living room, laid down on the couch and thought. The dragon's nursery rhyme played through her mind as she drifted off to sleep.

She found herself standing in front of the humongous cloud-like dragon, in all its glory, with her hands shielding her eyes from its brightness. Its stake like teeth were stained with blood that dripped down over its snarling mouth. A bloody Opal Amulet hung around its thick scaly neck. She noticed a small cave, just beyond where she stood, was being used as a holding cell. Inside the cave were some of the missing dragons. She wondered if Andrea or Aaron was amongst them; she was relieved and worried at the same time when she realized they weren't. The young dragons held captive looked unsure and they huddled together to keep warm.

Their legs were clasped with large thick bracelets, which looked like iron or steel rings interconnected in different sizes. Upon further observation she realized they were all chained together by manacles, not bracelets. Kyra shifted her steely gaze back on the white, cloudlike, dragon; he was watching her with keen interest; his eyes gleamed like lumps of burning coal.

"*Why?*" she asked him with her mind, gazing into his coal black eyes. "*Why?*"

Kyra stood transfixed as the white dragons mouth opened wider and wider and his jaws snapped down towards her. She jumped back and screamed. She threw her arms over her head shielding herself from his bite, waiting for the warmth of her blood to spill over her as she sat on the icy snow covered ground. Nothing came; only the thunderous ripple of his powerful voice. She peeked through her arms and could see he was shaking with laughter.

"Did you really think I could eat you in your dreams little girl?" He growled; his ebony eyes a mix of amusement and anger. "I only wish I were that powerful, you pathetic little human child?"

Chapter 9
QUEST FOR KNOWLEDGE

Kyra woke up still groggy and stared out the window at the bright, glittering, flakes of snow that were falling gently from the sky. Her mother was sitting quietly in the chair next to her reading. Kyra sat up and her mother looked up from her reading and smiled.

"You were sleeping for quite a long time," her mother said, getting up from her chair and going to her. "Are you hungry honey? Would you like something to drink?"

She gently placed a loving hand on Kyra's forehead and checked her temperature. Kyra had learned at school that you couldn't judge temperature by placing a hand on the forehead.

But it seemed to give her mother comfort in doing it that way. Her mother looked at her and smiled lovingly; seeming satisfied that Kyra was not running a fever. Kyra glanced out the window once more trying to decipher the time from the amount of light outside, but with the snow and clouds she hadn't a clue.

"What time is it anyways?" She asked her mother.

"You've been out for almost four hours; it's three in the afternoon. If you were thinking about calling your friends for the homework assignments they should be home by now."

She kissed Kyra on the forehead and headed towards the kitchen.

"I'll make us some soup and sandwiches, okay?" Her mother didn't wait for a reply. "Lunch will be ready in a jiffy."

Kyra lay on the couch listening to the clanging of pots pans and silverware; she knew her mother would have something hot and delicious in no time. She stretched out on the couch and thought about her experience. She thought about the nursery rhyme, the banished dragons, Andrea's little brother, Matthew, and the white dragon.

"Andrea!" Kyra called with her mind. *"Andrea, can you hear me? Please answer me. I need to know you're safe."*

The doorbell rang interrupting Kyra's thoughts.

"Now who could that be?" her mother said, hustling past Kyra to open the door.

Kyra heard her mother talking and then saying, "Come in, come in."

Andrea, an older man and a few other people entered the house, walked into the living room and stood in front of Kyra. She recognized some of them from that first night out on Barkers Island with Aaron.

"Sit down please, make yourselves at home," her mother said, grinning as she motioned to the guests with a sweep of her arm.

Andrea made introductions as soon as they all sat down in the living room. Kyra was so enthralled by the older man that she didn't hear when Andrea had introduced everyone. But when she introduced the older gentleman as Gustaf Duvos, Kyra was all ears. Gustaf was Aaron and Andrea's grandfather. Kyra nodded and smiled politely at him, but she couldn't help feeling afraid. She wasn't sure if he was there as a friend or foe. She wondered if the others were his prisoners. If he tried to attack she was ready to yell out for her mother to run; knowing full well that instead of running away from trouble her mother would run to protect her. Kyra wondered what the old man wanted. She watched Duvos get up from his chair and walk into the kitchen. She wanted to follow him, but Andrea grabbed her by the arm and bid her not too. Kyra pulled away from Andrea's grip and started to protest when her mother and Duvos came out of the kitchen laughing like old friends.

"A weekend retreat, at a farm," her mother said. "The doctor did say some rest and relaxation would do her good and she loves being out in the country."

They both laughed heartily, but her mom looked as if she might be hiding something.

"Well then, it's agreed!" Duvos said, smiling. "I promise you, I'll take good care of her. My granddaughter and grandson think the world of Kyra and I think Kyra feels the same way. I know my daughter will love having the company this time of year."

Her mother usually talked to her father about her excursions away from home, but he was away on leave so it didn't matter.

Kyra didn't have time to protest; her mother and Andrea hurried her upstairs to pack for a weekend in the country. Andrea rummaged through Kyra's dresser drawers pulling out jeans, sweatshirts, T-shirts and some warm thick socks.

"Pack warm!" Andrea laughed, ignoring Kyra's grumbles. "Do you have snow pants? Oh and don't forget boots, mittens, scarves and a hat. You'll need it where were going."

"Where are we going," Kyra asked, sarcastically. "To the Artic Circle?"

Andrea grinned, picked up Kyra's overstuffed luggage and started for the door.

"Don't just stand there," she said. "We have to hurry."

Kyra grabbed everything she needed and followed closely behind Andrea.

She didn't trust Gustaf Duvos or his quirky smile. Her mother, on the other hand, seemed to trusts almost anybody. She was letting Kyra go off on a weekend with a total stranger, but she had no way of knowing that these people were dragons. Duvos had put some sort of dragon magic on her mother, hypnotizing her into letting Kyra go with them. The whole group left the house and got into a waiting van.

"Mom, I don't want to go," Kyra pleaded. Her eyes were misty and red.

"Now Kyra, I think the country will be beneficial to you," her mother said, reassuringly. "You'll see."

"Bye mom, I'll miss you."

Her mother's eyes filled with tears. She leaned into the van and kissed Kyra on the cheek.

"Be safe, I'll see you soon."

"I love you mom!" Kyra shouted out the window as they drove off.

The van roared off, tires crunching through the snow, leading her into the unknown. Music from the radio was a steady din against the chatter. Andrea was sitting next to Kyra. She was talking to her cousin Bill; a husky auburn haired boy Kyra had seen occasionally in the halls at school. She wasn't interested in their conversation; she was lost in thought, staring out the window, trying to memorize each twist and turn of their journey.

"Kyra?" Andrea said, nudging sharply to get her attention.

"Huh?" Kyra said, blinking her eyes and focusing her attention on Andrea.

"I'm sorry."

"For what?"

"I wanted to tell you more before we left," she said apologetically. "It's just that we had to hurry."

"You looked scared when we were leaving," Bill said, on cue. "We weren't trying to scare you. We're trying to help you."

Kyra watched Bill's eyes, studied his body language and listened to the sound of his voice; trying to see if he was lying, but she didn't think he was.

"I'm not too sure about that?" Kyra said, indignantly. "Sometime before you arrived there was a white dragon peeking in my window. I thought he was going to eat me!"

"A white dragon?" Andrea asked.

"Yes. He was snarling like he wanted to take a bite out of me,"

"He was just probably curious about whom you were and I bet he was really smiling at you," Andrea offered, but she knew it was really more to what she was saying.

Kyra nodded solemnly and then she started laughing and thinking about how the white dragon was smiling at her. Her stomach rumbled loudly and the sound echoed through the van. Andrea and Bill covered their mouths with both hands, trying to hide their laughter.

"Here," Bill said, handing her a bright green apple and trying to keep a straight face.

Kyra had missed lunch and she wasn't going to wait to see if he would retract his offer. She grabbed the apple swiftly from his hand and devoured huge chunks.

"Wow, you eat almost like a dragon!" Bill teased.

Bill and Andrea didn't seem to mind all the noise she was making; in fact, they enjoyed it! Mimicking her and laughing with each bite she took.

"Don't eat the core!" they teased in unison.

They took turns explaining to Kyra about what was known as, *The Farm*.

The Farm was a place of refuge for the dragons. On the farm, they raised turkeys, sheep, cattle and other livestock. They also planted vegetables. They even had their own make shift hospital. Their main concern, however, came from the humans who trespassed during deer hunting season.

"There's nothing more dangerous than some trigger happy hunter with a gun," Bill said grudgingly. "One day we were sitting out on the porch, practicing how quickly we could turn into dragons, when POW, a bullet ricocheted off Aaron's back and logged into the side of the house. The hunter thinking he shot a deer was startled to see a bunch of kids sitting when he walked over to claim his prize. He didn't even ask if we were Okay, instead he asked if we seen an injured deer go by.

It wasn't until Aunt Thaliana came out with a huge cast iron skillet, waving it around and pointing to the side of the house that he realized he might have shot one of us. Well, technically, he did, but a bullet from a shotgun to a dragon is like a grain of sand to a human. The rest of us, still in human form, however, might have been killed. In human form, we are as vulnerable as humans. Anyways he apologized profusely and Aunt Thaliana escorted him all the way off her land by his ear; she was fuming all the way! Boy, was he shocked when he figured out she was blind!"

"Andrea, if your mother is blind how was she able to lead the hunter off the property?" Kyra asked.

"Close your eyes Kyra and I'll show you," Andrea whispered warmly.

Kyra closed her eyes and visions of icy snow top-mountain ranges appeared; it looked as if she was flying over them. The wind seemed so real; she shivered a little in response.

"Where is this?" she asked. Her eyes were still closed and she was enjoying the view.

"The Himalayan's," Andrea replied. "The process at which you are able to visualize images is called *think-a-vision*."

When Andrea stopped transmitting her plasma wave at Kyra, the images in her mind faded. She sat back and smiled in wonder at what she had seen.

"Wow!" She said elatedly. "That was fantastic. Can you do it again?"

"Not right now," Andrea said, somewhat exhausted. "It takes a lot of energy to produce images of that magnitude, maybe later."

"Never mind that Kyra," Bill said, giving Andrea a dirty look. "As I was saying before I was so rudely interrupted.

After the shooting, Aunt Thaliana made us all go out and put up signs that read, No trespassing. Violators will be eaten on sight. The locals thought the signs were funny, but they didn't know how serious my Aunt Thaliana really was."

"I thought you weren't supposed to eat humans?" Kyra said trying for a laugh, but no one responded.

"Oh, it wasn't us who were going to eat them," Bill said. "There are other creatures in the woods like werewolves and vampires; you know the usual woodland creatures."

Kyra smiled mockingly at Bill.

"Oh ya, you're right. I don't know why I would forget the usual woodland creatures like vampires and werewolves." Kyra said, sarcastically. "Let's not forget the trolls, fairies, elves and pixies. Then there's Bigfoot, unicorns, witches and wizards too! If you're trying to scare me forget about it buddy! I've been around the block a few times."

"Kyra," Andrea said, without as much as a smile. "He's telling the truth."

Kyra's face reddened and her mouth fell open.

"Truth? He's telling the truth?"

"Yes. The Farm is not only a refuge for dragons, but other creatures as well. They don't usually bother us and we don't bother them."

"You didn't tell me you lived out here; you said you lived a few blocks from my house."

"I do, but that's my uncle and aunts house. They're Bills parents and Bill, as I told you, is my cousin."

"Oh," Kyra said, a bit dumbfounded.

"Can you imagine being a blind dragon? Since we are dragons first and not human, being blind creates a sundry of challenges for my mother.

We dragons fly by sight, not sonar like bats, so it's difficult for her to see where she is going, unless someone is there to guide her with *think-a-vision*, and even then it is very difficult. Humans have specially made items for the blind to navigate in your world. Stoplights, for instance, have a pinging sound to let blind people hear when it's safe to cross. There are no such devices for dragons."

Kyra remembered Aaron, the first day they met, his glowing brown eyes and him sitting proudly in his wheelchair.

"So, she's kind of like Aaron, but she's able to see when the moon is out, right?"

Andrea looked at Bill and nodded.

"The effect the moon has on Aaron is only temporary," Bill said. "Eventually the debilitation Aaron and Thaliana suffer from will become permanent. There aren't any wheelchairs for dragons, nor would building one be feasible; we are much too big. Aaron will still be able to fly and use his wings to help him get around, but as a human he will be bound to his wheelchair for the rest of his natural days."

"Kyra," Andrea said. "As dragons we are protected from many things, but in human form we carry the same traits as humans."

Kyra didn't know what to say, even being human; no two people experience life the same way.

"Look Kyra," Andrea's voice chimed. "We're almost there." She reached out and squeezed Kyra's hand in anticipation. "I can't wait to see my mom!"

Kyra looked out the window; the vans headlights were the only visible light. The van bounced and shifted with every bump and turn; the beam from the headlights reflecting against the snowy ground.

Large evergreens, oaks and birch trees reminded her of scenic picture postcards. Kyra's stomach became queasy when she thought she saw flittering shapes scurrying along beside them, keeping pace with the van; she unconsciously backed away from the window, but not before a massive figure loom up unexpectedly close to her window. She jumped in her seat, knocking into Andrea and covered her mouth to stifle a scream.

"Don't worry Kyra," Andrea assured her. "It's only Bob Bigfoot, out on his evening prowl with his wife, Bobette."

Oh, I see," Kyra said sarcastically. "It's only Bob and Bobette Bigfoot. What ever happened to the vampires and werewolves?"

No sooner had she spoke the words, as if on queue, a howl reverberated deep in the night.

Kyra shivered in her boots.

Great, I'm behaving like a cockroach, she thought. *Screaming and scurrying for cover at the first sign of what could be a threat. I think cockroaches would scream if they could and maybe they do, but we just can't hear them. But my momma didn't raise me to be no cockroach!*

Chapter 10
THE FARM

The van cruised up in front of a large log cabin; it was a four-story log building, with a huge roofed porch that rapped around the entire house. There were large terraces at almost every window and an array of chimneys cascading up towards the sky from the roof. The bright glow from the porch lights cast a warm blush around the figure of a small woman and a very large man. The pair ambled out from sliding glass double doors and floated down the steps towards the van. The petite woman waved merrily as Gustaf opened his door and ambled out into the icy night air. The lights reflected on her short wavy ebony hair.

Her face was dainty and very feminine with large soulful looking eyes, but not so large they didn't fit her face. She was wearing the latest jeans, topped off by a regal blue sweater and black boots.

"Greetings," the small woman chirped happily. "I thought you would never get here."

She reached out her arms toward Gustaf. They hugged quickly, patting each other on the back. The ample man standing next to her made her look like a small child. He wasn't only huge, but had sharp features with a hairy face and arms; he was a muscular man with tight fitting pants and a loose fitting top. The big man grimaced as Gustaf reached out and attempted to shake his hand.

"How you doing 'old man," Gustaf said, warmly.

"Humph," he grunted, frowning a little, as he reached out, shaking Gustaf's small hand.

Andrea, Bill and Kyra climbed slowly out of the van behind the other passengers. The sky above them was filled with winking stars and the reddish glow of the moon. The air was crisp with the coming winter, fogging each breath they released back into the chilly air. Snow crunched under their feet, leaving a distorted path as they scurried, with Kyra in tow, to greet Andrea's mother; the infamous Aunt Thaliana. Kyra wondered if the large man was somehow another relative.

"Aunt Thaliana!" Bill called out as he embraced her in his arms.

"Bill, my little darling, so good of you to come all this way to see your Aunt," she cooed, stretching on her toes and giving him a light kiss on both cheeks.

"And who do we have here?" she asked, looking at Kyra. "Could this be our famous Kyra?"

Kyra's jaw looked unhinged as she stared at Thaliana, knowing the woman couldn't really see her, but the shock of her knowing where she was standing was amazing. It was as if she knew what Kyra was feeling and thinking. Thaliana smiled and thought her voice gently into Kyra's head.

Sight-a-vision, my dear Kyra, compliments of my beautiful daughter.

"Kyra," she said, gently grasping her hand. "It's a pleasure to finally meet you."

Then with a swift fluid movement, Thaliana pulled Kyra into her arms hugging her as if she were one of her own.

"Uhm, nice to meet you too," Kyra mumbled, surprised by the warm greeting.

Thaliana released Kyra and stepped back; Kyra noticed that her eyes were the color of opals.

Gustaf and the large man hurried into the house; their voices were raised in some heated discussion.

"Mom," Andrea's voice softly called out as she wrapped her arms lovingly around her mother. "I missed you so much."

"Oh, Andrea I missed you too," her mother said, kissing her on both cheeks like she did Bill. "Let me look at you."

"I'll do the honors," said Bill. He stepped forward to get a better view of Andrea.

Thaliana lifted her hands up to touch Andrea's face. Slowly, methodically, her fingers traced Andrea's facial features.

"You look more and more like your grandma everyday!" She exclaimed, laughing. "I hope you're all famished. Andrea, you look as if you're not eating at all, well, I can remedy that. I made a big dinner for tonight and invited some of the usual guests."

Taking Andrea and Kyra by the arm, she led the two girls side by side into the grand house, with Bill trailing behind. The front foyer, of the grand log house, glowed with natural beauty; it was decorated with old world charms and collectables from the eighteen century. In the center of the domed ceiling hung a crystal chandelier that refracted the light like a prism; the colors it created danced and swayed around the room. On either side of the walls hung bright tapestries depicting different stories from the past. There was also an eclectic collection of carved dragons, made of fine polished cherry wood, sitting behind short glass cabinets.

"Beautiful, isn't it?" Thaliana asked Kyra, sensing that the sight of the grand room enthralled her with delight.

"Yes, but how did you know what I was thinking. Can you read my thoughts?"

Thaliana laughed and shook her head.

"I knew because it captivated me the first time I saw it. The chandelier is one of the key features of the foyer." She paused for a moment, a knowing smile beamed on her face. "Andrea, could you please show Kyra her room? I would think after that long trip you all would like to freshen up."

Kyra's cheeks were flush pink; she really did like the idea of freshening up before dinner. Andrea led Kyra down a long spacious hallway decorated with paintings and tapestries. The floor was so shiny that it looked like a wooden mirror, reflecting the walls and the ceilings in its glow. At the end of the large hallway was a swirling staircase fit for royalty and big enough to accommodate two dragons, climbing side by side, up the red-carpeted steps. At the top of the landing were many rooms. The girls walked along the landing, pass several doors, until they reached Kyra's room.

Andrea opened the door and the two went inside. There was a bed fit for a queen inside the large room, a vanity with mirror and a sitting area; it was complete with a small sofa, reading chair and lamp. Across from the sitting area were sliding glass doors that led to a large private terrace. There was also a large bathroom with a private shower, sink, commode and a nice size Jacuzzi. Kyra was doing the potty dance by the time Andrea finished showing her the room.

"It's a very nice room Andrea," Kyra said, still doing her little potty dance. "And I really appreciate you going to all the trouble showing it, but if you don't mind, I really have to go."

Andrea giggled.

"Okay Kyra," she said, smiling. "I'll be back after you've cleaned up to escort you down to dinner. Oh one last thing, your luggage is under the bed."

Alone at last! She thought.

Kyra ran to the bathroom, breathing a sigh of relief and then she took a quick shower afterwards and changed her clothes. Just as she had finished dressing there was a dull (womp-womp) sound on the door. It was a strange sound, but even stranger than that, with each womp, the lights blinked in unison. Kyra jumped and smeared her lip-gloss across the side of her face; she was startled by the strange sound and blinking lights.

"Kyra, are you going to answer this door or not!" Andrea's angry voice wafted through the thick wooden door.

"Just come in." Kyra called from the bathroom. She was putting the finishing touches on her hair and wiping the lip-gloss from her cheek.

"Aren't you ready yet?" Andrea said, standing behind her.

Bill was standing outside the room, leaning against the doorframe.

"As ready as I will ever be." Kyra said.

They left the room and walked the expanse of the landing to the stairs. Kyra stopped at the top of the stairs with a quizzical look in her eyes.

"Andrea, Bill," she said, in a mild tone. "The lights in my room blinked when you knocked on the door. Is that normal?"

Bill and Andrea looked at each other and grinned.

"I knew she would notice!" Bill said.

"The house is set up for all kinds of people." Andrea explained. "If a person had a hearing problem and couldn't hear when someone knocked on the door, the blinking lights would tell them that someone was knocking on at door."

Kyra's breathe a sigh of relief.

"I'm glad that's all it was," she said. "With all the strange things happening, I thought maybe someone was trying to reach me from the grave!"

The tension dissipated like the aroma of cheap cologne and they all had a good laugh. It felt good to be able to laugh with friends.

"Oh and just so you know. In the morning when your alarm goes off, your bed will vibrate too." Bill laughed.

"Anything else I should know?" Kyra asked.

"There's an elevator just down the hall and a panic button in your bathroom just in case you need—um—help."

Kyra promise herself that when she got back to her room she'd go about the business of checking the place to see what other contraptions lay hidden. The trio made their way down the swirled stair-way. Kyra could see a huge banquet hall located between two marble pillars, though everything around the grand house was built to accommodate dragons; she was still amazed by the sheer size of everything.

The three tables were made of polished red oak and big enough to seat at least a hundred people at each. The center of the tables each held and array of colorful casseroles, meats and vegetables. A side table, that skirted the far wall close to the kitchen, held a variety of desserts stacked as high as Kyra's head. She felt hungry enough to eat an assortment of the main courses and desserts to boot.

"Kyra." she heard someone whispering softly in her ear. The sound tickled her neck.

She closed her eyes tightly. *Could it be,* she thought. *I must be hearing things again.* Then she felt arms wrap around her from behind.

"Kyra," he said again. "I missed you."

"Aaron," she said, elatedly, her eyes were moist with tears.

She turned, wrapping him deeply in her arms. He stared at her with caramel colored eyes that studied her fine features. The sight of him filled her with warmth she had never known. He bent down and kissed her lightly on the lips. It was a caring, warm, kiss; as soft as flannel sheets on a cold winter's night. They gently relaxed their embrace and looked into each other's eyes.

"Where have you been?" Kyra asked lovingly.

"It's a long story," Aaron said. "But let's not talk about it now, dinner is about to be served."

Chapter 11
THE GUEST OF HONOR

Time for dinner everyone!" Bill announced, as the guests started seating themselves at the tables. Aaron expertly guided Kyra to their chairs, pulling her chair out for her to sit and then seated himself next to her. They held hands under the table as Thaliana spoke; her voice magnified by the acoustics of the room.

"I like to thank everyone for coming," she said as gracefully as a queen. "I hope you all enjoy the meal we've prepared for you with great care. After dinner we have some important business to discuss. So I would appreciate if you all stayed after the meal please."

When she had finished her speech, a title wave of noise erupted as the food rotated around the tables from person to person. Aaron made sure Kyra tried everything a human would eat. Some of the dishes he explained were off limits to her. She understood completely as she noticed a small group further down the table, pouring what looked like thick ruby red liquid into silver goblets. She watched as they sucked down the contents in the goblets greedily. One male, in the group, with curly short dark hair, turned and smiled at Kyra as she watched them raising their cup in a toast. Aaron nudged her sharply with his elbow then flashed his teeth in warning.

"Kyra, you need to be careful," he said, his eyes soft with concern. "The small group, your staring at, drinking from the silver goblets are vampires and extremely clever when it comes to getting a fresh meal. If you know what I mean."

Kyra seemed to hear his words from a distance as she gazed, almost hypnotized, into his big brown dreamy eyes.

Such beautiful eyes, she thought into his mind.

"Thank you, Kyra," he said, blushing. "But you really need to pay attention to what I'm telling you. On the farm here, they are protected and supposed to stay away from human blood, but if you flag yourself as bait to them, well, they could loose control and I wouldn't put it past any of them to want to take a bite out of you."

Without answering, she quickly diverted her eyes down at the food on her plate. She knew Aaron was probably right; he lived on The Farm and knew all about the residents living there. Kyra never felt so out of her environment as she did now. She watched the other guests carefully this time, noticing that the social structures were all different for each group.

She continued to look around at each table, not daring to meet anyone's gaze, she became aware of how everyone was on their best behavior; being careful with their actions so as not to entice or offend anyone at the dinner. Each group had their own special medallions, which they wore, to separate each individual group from the other.

"Aaron," Kyra whispered, hoping not to be heard. "Who are the people with the dragon medallions."?

He smiled broadly at her.

"They are witches and wizards," he said. "When we are all together like this, so many different creatures in one space, they act as mediators and if need be, police."

Kyra coughed and choked trying to keep her food down when a nasty smell penetrated her nostrils. The smell reminded her of a mixture of old sweat, horse manure and rotting garbage. She could see others doing the same, only the dragons seemed unaffected; while many of the other guests were covering their noses with cloths, napkins and a few were spraying something to cover up the awful smell. A small few ran from the table trying to salvage what they had eaten, but didn't succeed; globs of undigested food issued from their mouths and splashed onto the floor. Two very large and very hairy human like creatures walked into the dining area. They crossed the floor to the last two empty seats and sat down; sending most of the other guests scurrying away from them. The largest one looked around the table, shrugging its shoulders; it didn't understand what all the fuss was about. The coughing and gagging reached a crescendo. Thaliana stood up and spoke in a guttural language to the two hairy creatures. The largest one responded in what sounded somewhat like an apology. Thaliana responded with another string of guttural sounds and then she smiled.

Aaron leaned over to Kyra and laughed.

"Bob says he was sorry for the chaos they caused; he and his mate had a difficult time finding someone to watch their children and didn't have time to bathe."

Thaliana stood up, smiled and with a slight movement of her hand motioned to a man sitting beside her. One of the wizards stood up, cloaked in a white cape, a dragon medallion shimmered against his chest, and chanted an incantation. The odor disappeared and the two hairy creatures looked much cleaner.

My dinner is saved! Kyra thought.

She did, however, still feel a little green in the face from the odor. The guests that left the table came back looking a little haggard and greeted the two new guests with nods and smiles. Those with appetites resumed their eating while the rest just sat and chatted. Aaron got up and went over to the dessert table; bringing back with him a heaping plate of sugary goodness. The two of them took turns feeding each other bites of each dessert trying to decide which one was their favorite.

"Get a room!" Bill laughed as he walked up behind Aaron and Kyra, with Andrea beside him. "So, Aaron ole' buddy, cousin of mine, what happened to you? You just disappeared on us."

Aaron sighed, pushing back his chair.

"There's not much to tell."

"Try us anyways. You had us going out of our minds with worry. I think you owe us that much."

Aaron nodded wearily and began.

"The day before I was attacked, I put a note in the *Norse Mythology* book and slipped it into Kyra's backpack in hopes she'd find it.

But I realized she knew nothing of the book or the note when I had seen her. The night Kyra and I left Canal Park I sensed that someone was watching us and maybe even following us. At first, I thought it might be one of you spying on us, but after I dropped Kyra at her house I wasn't so sure. The essence I felt was dark; not the light that all of you emit. I wanted to make sure that Kyra was safe, so I flew around her house for a few hours that night, watching and waiting to see if the presence that I felt would reveal itself, but it hadn't and I thought maybe I was just being paranoid. When I decided to leave and fly home I was attacked in the air. I thought maybe I angered some birds because the shape of the thing was white and misty, but when I tried to swat them away it cut into my hand and it true shape was revealed; it was a white cloud-like dragon."

Aaron looked at Andrea, picked up his cup from the table, took a long drink of water and then he continued.

"I thought it was our grandfather playing one of his tricks on me, but he wouldn't have played so rough. It was then that I realized the colors it bore were not the same as grandfathers. This white dragon was more like storm clouds rather than the bright white iridescent shine of our grandfather."

Aaron stopped for a moment, looking around the room as if he expected the white dragon to appear at any moment. When he was satisfied that everyone was still eating and not listening to him speaking he continued.

"I didn't want to endanger Kyra, but I was scared; the white dragon was at least twice my size! I flew down and tried to knock on her window. The white dragon grabbed me by my tail and sank his claws into me. I twisted and turned in the air; my only thoughts were of escaping.

But when that didn't work, I relaxed my body so much that he must have thought I passed out. Apparently my little trick worked because he loosened his grip; that was the opportunity I needed. I flew rapidly upwards, breaking his hold. I tried to make it to Bill and Andrea's house for help, but he was on me before I could reach them. I fell to the ground, changed into human form and ran for my life. Somehow I managed to escape. I laid low for a while and when I was sure the white dragon was gone, I changed back into a dragon and quickly flew out to the farm to warn the council. Aunt Thaliana had already heard my calls for help and sent grandfather to find me. I was so scared I didn't realize how badly I was injured until I started falling from the sky. Grandfather swooped down, caught me on his back and carried me the rest of the way to the farm. I don't remember much after that except I kept calling out to Kyra."

Aaron looked at Kyra and tenderly brushed her face with his fingers.

"I'm sorry Kyra; it was because of me you passed out in school. In the short time we have been together, our mental bond has become strong; when I called out your name in pain that pain was transmitted to you as well."

Aaron's face was downcast and dark as if he was guilty of a hideous crime, but Kyra knew it was an innocent mistake. She reached out to him and held his hand gently in hers. Then she tilted his face up with her other to meet her kindly gaze.

"Aaron its okay, you didn't know what you were doing. I'm glad you trusted me enough to call out to me."

He pulled away from her, his eyes misty and face serious.

"Kyra, I could have killed you," he said. "You're not a dragon. The injuries I suffered might have killed a human.

If it hadn't been for Aunt Thaliana filtering my thoughts, the pain I was conveying to you might have been fatal."

"Hey!" Andrea interrupted. "She wasn't the only one you were sending them to cousin!"

Kyra, gave Andrea a scolding glare and then she focused her attention back on Aaron.

"Aaron," Kyra said, wispily looking deeply into his caramel colored eyes. "Everything turned out fine. I understand what happened. Besides, if I'm *the one*, I'm sure I can handle it."

A single tear drifted down his chiseled cheeks.

"What happens if we're wrong and you're not *the one*?"

Chapter 12
THE MEETING

"Everyone sit down please!" Thaliana's voice echoed through the dining hall. The guests were full and maybe some still a little queasy after the great stench that had engulfed the hall and was defused by a wizard. Rumors filled the hall with murmurs, of a rogue dragon, the missing youth torn out of the sky and disappearing into oblivion. Others had no clue of what was going on or why they were there; they only knew that they had been summoned by the great lady herself, Thaliana. The guest voices ranged from quiet confusion to interest to outright anger and rebuttal. Some even felt that whatever troubles or concerns the dragons had they should just keep it to themselves.

Bill, Andrea, Aaron and Kyra all sat down together; all waiting to hear Thaliana's speak. Aaron wanted to talk to Kyra privately. Bill and Andrea just wanted some sleep and Kyra, still weary from the long trip, couldn't wait to try out the Jacuzzi in her bedroom.

"Let the meeting begin!" the large man sitting next to Thaliana said. When he spoke, all the chatter in the banquet hall had ceased abruptly.

Kyra leaned over to ask Aaron who the large man was. About the same time Thaliana stood up regally and asked Aaron to come to the front of the room. She was wearing a turquoise blue evening gown that blended into the soft light of the room; she looked more striking than ever. Aaron stood up immediately and calmly walked to the front of the room. On the way he turned and sneered at the vampire who had stared at Kyra, earlier in the evening, as a warning to stay away. Aaron was clad in blue denim jeans and black over sized t-shirt under an open black button down tailored shirt. The outfit defined his lithe muscular frame and highlighted his golden brown eyes. Thaliana greeted him with a warm hug and kissed both his cheeks. Aaron returned the gesture before the two turned and addressed the audience. The guest shifted somewhat restlessly in their seats, waiting. Thaliana sat in her chair, giving Aaron the floor. He cleared his throat and glanced over at Kyra, Bill and Andrea for support. Bill was the first to give Aaron a quick thumbs up and Andrea followed his lead. Kyra blew Aaron a kiss and Aaron reached out, pretending to grab it, and lightly touched it to his lips.

"Can we get on with this?" someone yelled.

Aaron looked over at Thaliana; she nodded and he began to recount the ordeal of his plight at the hands of the white dragon.

When he finished his tale, the vampire Aaron sneered at stood up and voiced his opinion.

"What does this have to do with all of us?" he asked. "None of us attacked him, it was one of you!"

Thaliana frowned, stood up and confronted his words. Aaron skirted the crowd and sat down solemnly by Kyra. She felt for his hand under the table and accidentally touched his upper leg. Her face gleamed red. Aaron laughed as the red slowly subsided from her face. He grasped her hand and gave it a soft squeeze then they turned there attention back to the front of the room.

"It concerns us ALL!" Thaliana said. "The dragon that attacked Aaron was no ordinary dragon. He was one of the *originally banished dragons*."

Her voice echoed loudly through the room, under towed by a buzz of voices that grew in volume until it was difficult to distinguish the sound as speech.

"HUSH!" the huge man ordered, coming to her rescue; his eyes ablaze and he was staring down at anyone who dared to disobey his command.

Thaliana smiled at him warmly before continuing.

"Many of you have already speculated what this means to all of us here at the farm as well as the human communities. If the white dragon is bold enough to travel so far out of his territory to attack a youngling, he is capable of ANYTHING! No one will be safe from his wrath, especially if he convinces the other banished to follow him."

The crowd was growing restless and many guests nodded in agreement. Some stared at Thaliana with contempt. They were sitting on the edge of their seats ready to pounce if needed.

"I see some of you agree with me. Some of you are old enough to know how the dragons came to North America and others are not. So, for those of you who do not, I would like to tell you a story."

When dragons and humans first existed there was a family originally called the Tostensen's who later generations became the Pedersen's; they were considered 'the ones'. When the Tostensen's first claimed the land they farmed, the family found a small clutch of dragon eggs; instead of destroying them or selling them, the family incubated the eggs until they hatched and raised the dragons as their equals. As the dragons grew, the Tostensen's were having difficulties keeping up with their appetites, so a few of the young dragons set out on their own. Each one returned with their mate to lay their eggs and stayed until the eggs hatched before moving on once again. The ones who remained protected the family from attacks and other predators. Generation after generation growing up with dragons they were able to speak to each other and both dragon and human considered themselves family.

The time came where Pedersen's farm was no longer safe for their dragon family. The Dragon king fearing possible extinction went to the Petersen's for help, asking if they would take a treacherous secret voyage to find a safe haven for their last clutch of dragon eggs and a few dragons that would watch over the eggs and them across the seas. 'The Ones' agreed, loading their boat with provisions and the dragon eggs, set out across previously uncharted seas to find a safe haven for their dragon kin.

They sailed for months across the ocean guided by the stars, stopping on land every now and then to rest, hunt and repair their boat. When they were exhausted and near starvation the dragons that followed chortled and helped guide the boat into a safe harbor. The land was lush and green. Filled with birds and other animals the dragons could hunt for food. There were cliffs by the sea that offered a secure place for the dragon eggs to be stored until they were ready to hatch. The Petersen's job accomplished; they said goodbye to their dragon brethren before departing to sail back to their homeland, leaving them to live in peace, in what is now, North America.

As the original dragon's population grew, they created the pact of three. Firstly, they would never eat humans again. Secondly, they would live in human form, rather than dragon form, when among humans. Thirdly, the dragons would try to abide by human ways in order to survive in peace. Most dragons agreed but a few of the older and bold young ones would not abide by the pact of three; therefore they were banished into the farthest reaches of the north where humans usually did not reside. Before the dragons could be banished however, they went on a rampage, led by a great white dragon, killing and devouring as many humans and creatures like all of you before they were driven away. While many dragons died on both sides, the great white dragon survived and has survived miraculously for thousands of years. Over these thousands of years, it is said the great white dragon is building a vast army, waiting for an opportunity to reclaim what he feels belongs to the banished and make humans, and anything resembling them, pay for the end of the 'reign of dragons,' as top predators, and pay they will, with their lives.

The great white dragon, Grackle as he calls himself, is the Dragon Kings youngest son.

The hall was silent, no one dared speak; this story was not a fabrication, but all too real. Kyra knew enough about dragon folklore to know what a formable foe an ancient dragon could be.

How had Grackle stayed alive all these years? She thought.

As if Gustaf heard Kyra's question, he stood up and nobly walked to the front of the room. All eyes followed him, as he stood there before the audience, in his blue denim overalls, looking more distinguish than many of the guests. Average in height, his eyes as blue and crisp as the sea with shocking white short cut hair; the lines on his face, from age only, added to the affect; he knew it wasn't always what one wore, but how one wore it and carried ones-self. He placed a fatherly arm around Thaliana, leaning over and whispering something in her ear that made her grin. He removed his arm from around his daughter, took a couple steps forward, grasped his hands in front of him and began.

"I have never seen the white dragon myself," his rich voice boomed, drowning out any noise from the crowd.

The guests shifted in their seats but nobody said a word.

"It is said he wear's an opal amulet around his neck, giving him the power of regeneration. Our council believes that the opal amulet was created by a great wizard originally as a gift to the Dragon King and stolen by his youngest son before leaving for the *New World*."

All was eerily silent for moment, as if someone cast a spell over the crowd, everyone's breath stopped, frozen like statues, as Gustaf words sunk into meaning. Then, as if the spell had dissipated, people rose from their seats.

They were shoving their chairs and shouting accusations as if the dragons had dragged them down to the very depths of Hades. Some of the others screamed questions in hopes of being heard over the din. Gustaf stepped back, not in retreat, as some might have thought, but to bring his daughter forward to be by his side. The two standing together formed an imposing pair that emulated both great wisdom and strength. Gustaf and Thaliana, in all their wisdom, stood silent; allowing the release of frustration, fear and anger to pass before continuing. Gustaf raised his arms over his head, palms forward, to quell the crowd.

"Calm down. Thaliana and I will try to answer some of your questions."

The first question he addressed was the story of *the ones*. He explained to the nervous crowd that for thousands of years, *the ones* special gift had been lost in most of their descendants. A few guests started to mutter, but quickly stopped when Gustaf raised his hands once more.

"Is there anyone still living who carries this special gift?" Someone in the crowd shouted.

"Yes," Gustaf replied. "There is one such person that carries this special gift and we are lucky to have that person amongst us, in this very room tonight."

The room erupted in a mix of speculation and shock. Some of the guest shouted in disbelief. Many of them that had sat throughout the whole discussion were now on their feet. Still others looked around the room quizzically and wondered who could it be?

"Who is it Gustaf?" someone shouted.

"Well," a skinny witch asked. "Are you going to tell us?"

Gustaf stretched out his arm and pointed directly at Kyra.

"Her!" a fat warlock said.

"She's so young," another added.

"Poppycock!" a distinguishing looking man said.

"It's a joke," still another said. "He thinks we're fools."

Kyra could only stare in disbelief. Just days ago she was an ordinary school girl, tormented and teased by her peers, now she was the center of attention. A thousand pair of eyes was set upon her. Kyra slouched down in her seat, trying to hide from their glaring eyes, hoping no one would notice, but she couldn't help hearing comments throughout the room.

"Enough!" Gustaf roared, the sound of his voice booming through the hall, stifling the jeers and howls of the guest. "This young girl has more than proven herself. She has met Grackle and survived!"

Gustaf's defense of Kyra just seemed to upset the guest even more as a steady rhythm of loud voices refueled the burning chaos; some of the guests stood defiantly, slamming their chairs in the process and stormed to the front of the room like a swarm of killer bees.

"You didn't tell us you saw Grackle at your window Kyra!" Aaron shouted loud enough to be heard over the ruckus.

Kyra looked confused; her brows knitted together, shoulders shrugged and eyes pleading. Even she was in disbelief over the revelation that it had been Grackle peering in her window that night and not Gustaf.

"I had no idea," Kyra said, somewhat dismayed. "I thought the white dragon was Gustaf not Grackle."

"You saw Grackle and lived?" Bill asked

Kyra nodded slowly, felling somewhat ill; not from the food she had eaten, but from the realization that she had met Grackle, the great White Dragon and lived to tell a about it.

She was immediately swarmed by hundreds of guest. They were pushing and shoving each other trying to get closer to her. The ones that managed to reach her smothered her with questions about the opal amulet. They wanted to know how big Grackle really was and how did she manage to survive. Aaron, Bill and Andrea tried to form a three-person blockade in an attempt to protect Kyra from the onslaught of guests that had crowded in around her.

Aaron and Bill started fearing for Kyra's safety as the onslaught of guests pawing at her grew out of control. The two boys quickly shifted into dragon form. The effect was immediate and the guests ran for cover. Andrea boosted Kyra safely up on Aaron's back and then she hopped gracefully onto Bills; they careened through the crowd, as carefully as possible, to avoid stepping on anyone by accident. Kyra wondered if Thaliana and Gustaf would frown upon the incident that had transpired. She was worried that she might have broken some sort of protocol, but when she turned to look over at them the pair was roaring with laughter. Now she thoroughly understood why everything was so huge; it was made especially for dragons. Aaron and Bill, a dragon the color of a golden sun, gracefully cantered out the banquet hall, up the swirling stairs and deposited Kyra safely at her bedroom door. Bill and Aaron quickly changed back into human form and followed Andrea and Kyra into the room; when they were all safe in the room, Bill skillfully locked the door behind them.

"Did you see their faces?" Bill said, laughing.

He laughed so hard he was crying; Aaron did too, but not for very long.

"Yes, but did you see that one of the vampires was trying to take advantage of the situation," Aaron said.

He wasn't laughing anymore.

"Ya, he was about to bite Kyra! I think he changed his mind when I stepped on his foot," Bill said, proud of his antics.

Aaron stared at Bill vacantly. Then he laughed harder than before.

"My heroes!" Kyra said in her most feminine voice. She reached up and gave Bill and Aaron a kiss on the cheek.

"Okay all ready!" Aaron said pulling away laughing. "So are you going to tell us about your run in with Grackle?"

Kyra jumped on the loft bed, motioning to the others to join her.

"Make yourselves comfortable," she said.

When Kyra finished her tale they all looked at each other as if unsure of what to say. The white dragon's sole purpose of visiting was to threaten Kyra, but how did he find her they wondered.

"Well, what do you think?" Kyra asked.

She watched them, as their eyes darted back and forth to one another as if they were having a conversation without her. She got up and walked to the bathroom, looking back to see if anyone had noticed; if they did they didn't let on. She reentered the room, looking up to see if anything had change while she was gone, but it hadn't. They were still engrossed in their silent conversation. Kyra sighed, picked up a book that was on her nightstand and went to find a comfortable place to read it. The balcony would have been inviting if it hadn't been so nippy out that evening; so she settled on an overstuffed, oversized, chair in the sitting area of her room. She took a seat in the comfortable chair and opened the book to the first chapter.

The first line read, "She's weird!" Flusheria said flipping her wild hair as she turned to face Riana, her eyes cold and hard. "I wouldn't be surprised if she killed us all. You know she's crazy."

I don't know who writes this stuff but they need to find another job, she thought, filled with a sense of deja vu.

Kyra was well into the book when Andrea came over and tapped her on the shoulder.

"Aiii," Kyra screamed, her heart pounding in her chest.

She had just reached the part where the evil villain was reaching out to grab the unsuspecting heroine. With her hand over her heart, as if that would slow its pace, she turned around and looked at Andrea.

"Sorry I scared you," Andrea said, shrugging her shoulders.

"It's not your fault. I was engrossed in this book."

Andrea moved in front of Kyra's chair, took the book out of her hands and put it on the floor. Then she grabbed Kyra by her arms and pulled her to her feet.

"Come on, the boys and I have some things to tell you."

"It's about time," Kyra huffed.

"Ya, we'll get over it. I have a major headache from all the talking."

Andrea and Kyra joined the boys on the bed, forming a circle.

"The only thing we can think of is when you tried to think-speak to Andrea somehow in the process you connected to Grackle instead," Aaron said.

The others nodded in agreement.

"How could I connect to Grackle when I never met him before?" Kyra asked

"That's what we were wondering too," Andrea chimed in.

"When you met our grandfather you were thinking of a white dragon when you tried to warn me. You should have been only thinking of me. Understand?"

Kyra nodded wearily; she had been thinking of Andrea while she was fleeing the white dragon at the time.

"I guess it's like thinking one thing and doing another, right?"

"Close enough." Bill said.

They all looked tired, dark circles hung under their blood shot eyes. In a futile attempt to be funny, Aaron winked at Kyra and said, "How about you and me trying out your Jacuzzi together?"

"Ya, that ought to work," Bill whispered acidly under his breath.

"Why? Don't you have one of your own?" she spat playfully back at him, followed by a big yawn.

"Enough you two," Bill said. He and Andrea grabbed Aaron by his arms and started pulling him out of Kyra's room and laughing hysterically.

"You need your sleep Kyra," Andrea said pulling the door shut. "We'll see you in the morning. Goodnight."

"Goodnight!" Kyra called to them.

Andrea's voice drifted through the crack of the door.

"You're safe here, don't worry."

What's there to worry about, I have the greatest protection around, a house full of dragons.

The door shut with a soft click. Kyra ran and turned the lever quickly to lock it; alone at last, it was time for her to check out the Jacuzzi. The Jacuzzi was opulent with gold colored knobs and nozzles; the pulsating swirling water soothed her as she sank deeper and deeper into its foamy warmth.

I'm going to have to ask mom and dad to buy one of these for the house, she thought smiling.

Kyra watched the shifting pulsing water and became concerned when she started to see shapes within the swirls. She blinked her eyes a few times and the shapes were still there. She stared, curiously as a foamy dragon head emerged out of the frothy bubbles; its head lifting up and facing her; its mouth opened wide and with one lighting strike it swiftly enveloped her head. She screeched trying to pull her head away, only to find herself tightly trapped in the dark sharpness of its teeth.

Andrea! Aaron! Bill! HELP ME! Her mind shrieked out to them. Her heart pounded in her chest threatening to burst. She gasped for air, sweat poured down her face. The dragon head was gone almost as quickly as it had arrived.

Kyra stumbled, scrambling out of the tub, water dripping in rivets on the tiled floor, she crawled rapidly bruising her knees as she pulled the drain lever; thankful that the lever was on the edge of the Jacuzzi rather than at the bottom. Scooting back, what she felt was a safe distance from the draining Jacuzzi; she sat there with her knees up to her chest and arms hugging them tightly, until the last remnants of water and bubbles vanished down the drain. Shivering, she stood up and grabbed a near by towel and walked swiftly to the bathroom. Urgently she flicked the light switch, bathing the bathroom in a bright light, squinting while her eyes adjusted to their glare as she studied her reflection in the mirror. Kyra gasped when she noticed trickles of red encircling her neck. She found a washcloth on the sink to wipe the blood away. She watched as her image in the mirror warbled and the light in the bathroom dim as the shock of the event invaded her body.

Clinging to the edge of the sink, as her legs gave way, she lost her footing and tumbled to the floor, hitting her head against the toilet along the way. She lay there for a moment on the bare cold tile floor, naked and feeling as vulnerable as the day she was born.

"Great!" She mumbled to herself, feeling a large lump that had formed on her head. "What more could happen to me?"

Kyra got to her feet and stumbled out of the bathroom to her bed. She lay down on her bed tired and weary; she snuggled deep into the softness of plush quilts, pulling the covers tightly around her. She could hear voices singing in the still of the evening air, *Chomp one, chomp two, chomp three, chomp four, until they're knocking at your door.*

She started to hum along; dreamily staring into the quiet dimness of her room. The lights flickered when she heard someone rap loudly on her bedroom door. Slowly she got up and staggered sleepily towards the door. She flipped the lock and clumsily opened it. Suddenly there was a *'swoosh'* and then everything went dark.

Chapter 13
THE FOUNDLING

Kyra awoke; home in her bed, to what sounded like a rampant chain saw; she was confused and disoriented. She remembered answering the door in her room at The Farm, but everything after that was a blur. A blush cascaded across her cheeks when she recalled she had been naked. *Naked!* Her mind screamed. Horrified, that maybe it had been Bill, Aaron or even Gustaf who might had brought her home, or maybe even some other man. She peeked under the covers and was relieved when she saw someone had dressed her in her pajamas. Then she was mortified when she saw her pajamas were covered in brown bristly hair. There was suddenly a burst of noise.

The walls were wobbling as if someone was using a jackhammer; knickknacks, books and stuffed animals crashed to the floor, sending Kyra scrambling out of her bedroom and out into the hallway.

"Earthquake," she screamed. "Mom, I think we're having an earthquake!"

The noise and the trembling crested like waves; she was pelted with pictures that were on the walls in the hallway. She crouched and tried to shield herself from the chaos. Her ears followed the rise and fall of the sound; sharp shards of glass were strewed all around her. Slowly she climbed to her feet, hanging on to the wall for support. With her first calculated step she missed a large thin shard with her toes and clipped it with her heal when she put her foot down.

"Ouch!"

She raised her foot and pulled a large thin slice of glass from her heel. A thin bead of blood washed down from a pinprick size wound.

"Mom, where are you!" she called.

The roaring and shaking continued, she laughed nervously, thinking the sound reminded her of when her father was snoring only ten times louder and more destructive. She was worried when her mother didn't answer so she checked the upstairs rooms first, to see if everything was all right. Since she was almost in front of her parent's bedroom door, she wove around the glass that littered the floor, until she was standing in the doorway scanning the room. The bed was neatly made like a picture in a catalog; soiled clothes filled the hamper in the corner, with the exception of the clutter on the floor that must have fallen off the dresser from the vibrations. The room was void of life; or perhaps her mother was hiding under the bed.

"Mom, are you in here?" she asked.

She stood on her toes swaying in the doorway, listening for sounds other than the thunderous grinding and rumbling that surrounded her. Satisfied her mother wasn't in the bedroom she moved on to the guest room.

"Mom."

"Oh hi honey, you're up early," her mother said blocking the entrance to the guest room, oblivious to the destruction that lay around her.

"Mom, what's happening?"

Her mother's eyes were wide.

"What noise? I don't hear anything." Then, as if she had noticed the wreckage for the first time she said, "That's the last time I buy cheap nails!"

Kyra could only stare in disbelief. *Had her mother finally lost it?* She thought.

"Mom, you know what I am talking about!"

"Oh that," she said, smacking her forehead lightly. "Oh that's just some guest we have, Bob and Bobette."

"Bob and Bobette? Who are they and how can they make such a horrible noise?"

"Well honey," her mom said, as she led Kyra away from the door and down the stairs. "Some people snore, they can't help it."

Kyra darted around her mother, ducking as she tried to grab her and threw the guest bedroom door open. She was shocked to see two sets of hairy feet hanging over the edge of the bed. They were two extremely large and furry Bigfoot she had seen at the dinner on the farm.

"What are they doing here?" she said, as another rattle, roar and blast of putrid breath surged around her.

She covered her mouth, gagging on the stench, her lungs calling for fresh air. They both sat up, blinking their big brown eyes and stared at her inquisitively.

"Um, hi Bob and Bobette," Kyra said mortified. "Um sorry to wake you, bye."

She waved at them and then she quickly shut the door, before they let go with another blast of rancid breath.

"MOM! What are they doing here?"

Her mother grinned and shrugged her shoulders.

"I told you we had guests. Let's talk downstairs."

The two descended the stairs and walked into the sunny kitchen.

"Mom!"

"Just a minute honey," her mother said, when the doorbell rang.

She peeked through the curtain.

"It's Grammy," she said. "Of all the days to visit, she had to visit today."

Kyra snickered when she thought of what Grammy's reaction might be if one or both of the Bigfoot came downstairs and walked into the kitchen.

Kyra's mother unlocked the door and Grammy walked in.

"Hi Grammy," Kyra greeted.

"Hi sweetheart," her grandmother replied.

Kyra's Grammy walked over and gave her a sloppy kiss on the cheek before sitting down at the table. Kyra's mom had poured Grammy a cup of coffee and sat it on the table.

"Would you like anything else?"

Grammy shook her head, took a sip of her coffee and sat the cup down with her hands still hugging it.

"We have to talk," Grammy said to Kyra, shifting in her chair and making herself more comfortable.

"Mom, Grammy, its ok. Don't worry. I know why we're all here together."

Her mother sat on the other side of Kyra.

"You do?" her mother said, relieved. "I wasn't sure if you knew or how we were going to tell you. Grammy only found out a few days ago."

A few days ago? I was psychologically disturbed a few days ago. She thought. *And I didn't even know it.*

"Kyra, are you all *right*?" Grammy asked, doing the old feel the forehead for a fever bit.

Kyra pulled away indignantly.

"I'm fine Grammy, just a little bewildered. Why you didn't tell me sooner? You know, so I could be a little more prepared."

The phone rang and her mother got up to answer it. She could hear her mother saying, "Oh yes, I'm sorry to worry you all, but she is here. I called Bob and Bobette to bring her home. I just felt it would be safer. I'll be looking forward to it. See you soon!"

Her mother hung up the phone and walked back into the kitchen.

"Was that Thaliana?" Grammy asked.

"Yes. She's going to come over later, after we're done with our discussion."

The three of them sat there, looking from one to the other, waiting for someone to speak.

"Kyra," Sunny said, a bit apprehensively.

"Sunny, are you going to start or not," Grammy scolded. "You're the so called expert on this."

"Ok, I'll start, but being the oldest in the family I would appropriate if you started by giving a brief family history first?"

"Okay," Grammy replied. "If you insist."

When Grammy had finished her tale about the dragons and *the ones,* Kyra nodded; she remembered each sequence of events in the saga. She was still mesmerized by how the dragons had come to North America.

"Do you remember that story Kyra?" Grammy asked.

"Yes Grammy. You told it to me many years ago."

"Well my dear," Grammy said, as she held Kyra's hand and sighed deeply. "The story is true."

Kyra smiled; the last few weeks were not an illusion after all, with the exception of Grackle, but then why were her mother and grandmother there.

"Grammy, do you know the rest of the story? What happened after the dragons settled here?"

Grammy and Sunny shook their heads and sighed deeply. They had no way of knowing the rest of the story as told by the dragons. Kyra shifted in her seat, eyes beaming, as she began to tell the Dragons side of the tale after *the ones* left them. The story Thaliana told at the meeting. They sat as still as statues, listening to the final piece of the saga, as Kyra finished.

Over these thousands of years, it is said the great white dragon is building an army waiting for an opportunity to reclaim what he feels belongs to the banished and to make humans and anything resembling them, pay for the end of the 'reign of dragons' as top predator and pay they will, with their lives. The great white dragon, Grackle as he calls himself, is the Dragon Kings youngest son.

She unconsciously added, *as the sun shall rise again, Grackle will fall and down will come the dragon lord pendent and all.*

Stunned by the added twist of words that came out of her mouth, she stared off into a far corner of the room; her mouth was slack and her eyes were wide in terror.

"What's wrong?" her mother asked.

"Mom, I don't know where that last sentence came from. I'm sure Thaliana didn't say that at the meeting."

Like a tennis ball volleyed on a court, she looked back and forth between her mother's steady gaze and Grammy's comforting face hoping one of them had the answer.

"Are you all right?" Grammy asked.

"Ya, just a little confused. Grammy, how did you get caught up in all this?"

"Well, to be truthful..."

"Let me tell her," Sunny said, interrupting.

"Okay," Grammy said. "If you insist."

"When I was a little girl I was having strange dreams about dragons. When I told your Grammy about the dreams she surprisingly told me that she was having the same dreams."

"That's when I decided to call some of our relatives," Grammy put in, "I asked them if they knew anything about the saga of *the ones*. Very few of them knew what I was talking about. I think they thought I finally lost my mind. It wasn't until I was doing some fall house cleaning when I found my fathers diary that he brought with him from Norway. I skimmed through the pages, you know I disliked reading of any kind, unless of course it happened to be the TV guide, and the word 'dragon' caught my eye. It was then I had to sit down and read it all.

"I wasn't sure how long I sat there reading that diary, but I do know I had missed my favorite TV show. For many years his diary had sat filed away unread, but here were the answers I had been looking for; from the words of a dead man. I devoured every word of that diary hungrily; looking for any other clues I might have missed and there it was. On a tattered folded page the same sentence that you had spoken. I didn't know what it meant until you told us the dragon's side of the saga. Those words hadn't made sense until now."

The three of them sat and stared at each other. They all realized that throughout their lives they had seen dragons flying, but they blocked it out of their minds for fear of being labeled crazy.

"I was a little shocked when I heard about you flying around with dragons. Thank God at least I know I'm not going senile yet!"

They all laughed until tears rolled down their cheeks.

"Hey?" Kyra asked. "How did you know I flew with dragons?"

Grammy covered her mouth with her hand.

"Oops, sorry," she said, looking guiltily at her daughter.

Kyra sat there, blinking slowly as her brain registered Grammy's unwitting confession. She was astonished that her mother knew about Aaron and still allowed her to go that night.

"You knew?" Kyra asked her mother.

"Yes, especially when I saw Andrea driving you home the first night."

"What about Andrea?"

"About twenty five years ago, I went to school with her. Some people you never forget. She and I were best friends. The weird thing about it all is she hasn't aged a bit."

Kyra understood why her mother let her go to The Farm so readily.

"Andrea and I had a sleep over at The Farm. It's quite a place isn't it?"

Kyra turned to her grandmother.

"Grammy, do you know Thaliana?"

"Yes. Your mom and I have had them over for dinner many times when your Grandpa Chuck was out of town on business."

"Wow, did you know they were dragons?"

"No your mother never cared to inform me of that."

Grammy sneered at her daughter as if she broke some cardinal rule by not telling her they had dragons over for dinner.

"So Kyra? This Aaron guy, is he nice?" Grammy asked.

"He's very nice Grammy."

Kyra shifted in her seat, not wanting to discuss Aaron. Her mother seemed to sense her discomfort.

"Oh, look at the time!" Sunny said, anxiously. "What do you girls want for lunch?"

Before Kyra could respond, Grammy said, "Well dear, I don't want to put you through any trouble so let's go out to eat, my treat!"

"I want to go to Bridgeman's!" Kyra said. "They have such fantastic malts and shakes. I might even try one of those lalapaloozas; it has tons of ice cream. If you eat it all they give you a button. Please Grammy, can we eat there?"

"Kyra you know the rules, healthy food before junk food."

"Ice cream is made out of milk and milk is healthy." Grammy added. "So let's go to Bridgeman's. Sunny you drive."

"Okay," Sunny said, giving in to their request. "Bridgman's it is, but I'm not having a lalapalooza. I'm watching my figure."

Grammy and Kyra monopolized the conversation on the drive to Bridgeman's. They talked about which kinds of shakes they were going to have and whether Kyra could eat a giant ten-scoop lallapalooza by herself.

"Sunny, what time did Thaliana say she would be at your house?" Grammy asked when they reached their destination and climbed out of the car.

"Later this afternoon," Sunny replied, as the three made their way into the restaurant.

Chapter 14
THE TRUTH BE TOLD

The three of them sat down for lunch, ordered and ate their meals. Kyra was so full of ice cream she felt ill. She had tried to eat a lalapalooza after finishing a cheeseburger and fries. Half way through her delectable ice cream treat her stomach started to protest. When she told her mother and Grammy she felt ill, her mother gave Grammy one of her 'I told you so' smiles and the two of them started shoveling pieces of pumpkin pie into their mouths speedily. They finished their pastry quickly in case Kyra suddenly decided to hurl. While they sat, they heard a gasp followed by a thunk of an overturned chair, at the table directly across from them.

"It was a dragon," A petite woman with red hair screamed. "I saw a white dragon in my whipping cream!"

The server and manager tried to calm the upset patron, but she continued her tirade, hoping that someone would believe her.

"It bit me!" she yelled. "Look."

She held out her hand to Kyra, Grammy and Sunny. They noticed that a tiny ring of red beads had formed on the woman's pinky finger.

"Grackle," they all whispered solemnly under their breaths.

The white dragon's magic had no bounds. He had the power to transcend his presence even into a mere cup of cocoa. The woman took their silence as confirmation that she indeed had been bitten and she was becoming more hysterical by the minute. An ambulance was called and when it arrived the woman was sedated and whisked away. Sunny, Grammy and Kyra watched as the ambulance sped off. Kyra couldn't help feeling sorry for the woman and they all knew she had been telling the truth.

"I feel sorry for her," Kyra said.

"Yes it's too bad," Grammy offered.

"Maybe we should have told them the truth," Sunny said.

"Told them what? That a white dragon named Grackle was spying on us and bit that poor lady in the process?"

"You're right; we would all be in that ambulance and on our way to the funny farm if we told the truth."

"Don't worry, she's in good hands," Grammy offered. "And I think it's time we left.

The three left the restaurant and went home. When they arrived home and walked into the kitchen Bob and Bobette where sitting at the table enjoying lunch.

Grammy wasn't too surprised seeing a pair of Bigfoot sitting at the table having lunch. If dragons were real, she figured, why not Bigfoot. The pair had consumed four boxes of cereal, a dozen bananas, twenty pop tarts, eight jars of peanut butter and a gallon of milk each. For desert they each had five fudge pops. Kyra wasn't sure if fudge pops were available out in the woods, where the Bigfoot lived, but they both seemed to like them. Kyra leaned closer, curious to see if they knew to add the milk to their cereal, but both bowls were empty and dry. She couldn't help laughing quietly at them as they looked at her innocently; she pushed the empty boxes onto the floor and grinned at them both.

"Houston, we have a problem," her mother said anxiously. She was standing there, bouncing her eyes between the cereal boxes on the floor and the Bob and Bobette's expression.

The term 'sugar rush' popped into Kyra's head as she followed her mother's pinging gaze. Never in her wildest dreams would she have ever thought that two large hairy creatures would be sitting at their table having a sugar fit. Bob and Bobette started pounding on the table, causing it to jump into the air.

"Think of something Kyra!" her mother said.

Grammy was standing in a corner laughing hysterically. She definitely wasn't going to be of any help unless she pulled herself together. Bob and Bobette got up and started chasing each other around the table whooping and hollering loudly. Kyra and her mother had to jump out the way to avoid being stepped on. Kyra stood pasted against the kitchen wall feeling as if she was on a trampoline as the weight of Bob and Bobette caused the floor to bounce erratically. Her mother was on the other side holding on to Grammy.

"Kyra!" her mom screamed over the noise of dishes falling out of the cupboards and crashing onto the kitchen floor. "Take them outside! If anyone asks, tell them they're your cousins from your father's side of the family. And don't let them leave the yard!"

My cousins, Kyra thought, someone would have to be idiotic to believe that one.

Kyra went into the cupboard pulled out a box of Puddily Pops and enticed the hairy beast to follow her outside. She took a quick and couldn't help seeing Grammy doubled over on the floor cackling with laughter at the situation.

"Oh... Sunny... ha ... you ...ha, ha, ha... throw ...ha, ha ...the wildest parties!" Kyra heard her Grammy stammer as she close the back door.

The three of them ran around the back yard playing tag. But for Kyra it was more like running for her life because the Bigfoot tagged so hard they knocked her down every time she was it. Nothing like a little cardiovascular fitness she thought as she scrambled frantically trying to out distance Bobette and avoid her bruising blow. She was sure that if she looked in the mirror she would be covered head to toe with purplish bruises. Bobette caught her, tagging her so forcefully on her back that she landed with her face implanted into the icy snow. Thinking maybe she'd should just lie there awhile and rest.

Bob became worried about her, laying face down in the snow, and before she knew it she found herself dangling in mid air by her ankle. Then, as if that wasn't enough, Bobette came over and poked her in the ribs a few times, checking to see if she was injured. When Bobette assured herself that Kyra was all right, she said something to Bob and he dropped her right back in the snow.

Kyra reached out her arms to break her fall and flipped over landing on her feet. Those gymnastic lessons really paid off. She watched the two of them running away from her. It was her turn to be it again. The three of them stood frozen in place when Gustaf's van suddenly turned awkwardly into the driveway. Kyra cringed and shielded her eyes when he almost clipped the backend of her mom's car with his bumper.

"You need a wider driveway" he called out happily, as he swung his door open.

Kyra gawked as his door stopped inches from slamming into the side of her mom's car. She wondered kiddingly if he was always this graceful as he walked around to the passenger's side, opened the door for Thaliana and helped her exit the vehicle. She could hear him giving Thaliana a thorough description of their backyard right down to where the snow covered sidewalk was. His words were a map to her ears; it allowed Thaliana to navigate her way to the backdoor.

"Bob and Bobette please come inside now before the neighbors get too curious." Thaliana said, extending her hand to them. "Come now."

She encouraged them when they did not move right away. Bob and Bobette pouted, unhappy their game was over, and walked slowly towards Thaliana.

"No pouting now."

She can't see them, so how did she know they were pouting, Kyra thought.

"I have my ways," Thaliana answered, reading Kyra's thoughts.

Kyra smiled. She had forgotten the magic Thaliana had possessed.

"Kyra," a voice called from behind. "Aren't you at least going to say hello."

"Aaron," she said, elatedly.

She spun around too quickly, slipped and fell on her backside. She could feel her face hot with embarrassment. She looked up and said jokingly, "Hey, Aaron. I've fallen for you."

Bill and Andrea were standing behind him laughing so hard they were snorting.

"That's a good one! Wasn't that a good one Aaron," Bill proclaimed, slapping him on the back. "Oh don't mind him. He's grouchy today. You should have seen him when he found out you were missing. We looked for you all night long you know."

"I'm sorry," she said guiltily, even though it hadn't been her fault. "I hadn't even known I was missing until I woke up at home this morning."

She had no idea her mother decided to get Bob and Bobette to kidnap her from 'The Farm' and carry her home. Andrea looked at Aaron's sulking figure and said, "I guess he's still a little sore about the whole thing."

Andrea scrunched up her nose and stuck her tongue out at Aaron behind his back causing Bill to stifle a laugh.

"I saw that!" Aaron blurted.

"What?" Andrea said, innocently walking in front of Aaron. "I didn't do anything. Let's go in Kyra, its getting a little chilly out here."

"What about Aaron and Bill?"

Kyra felt a little concerned leaving the boys outside.

"Well, if Aaron gets stuck in the snow, I'm sure his buddy Bill will help him out. Won't you Bill?"

"Uhm, ya sure." Bill stammered.

The kitchen was buzzing with conversation. Grammy, Thaliana, Gustaf and Kyra's mother sat at the table talking. Andrea went to see what Bob and Bobette where doing since she didn't see them around and Kyra stayed in the kitchen. She watched Thaliana speaking to her mother and Grammy and she thought it would be difficult for anyone to know Thaliana was blind. Kyra had never known a blind person before, but she could see no peculiarity in Thaliana's response or behavior. She guessed Thaliana just had a different way of seeing. A thousand thoughts filled her brain. She thought of Aaron; how he was unable to walk during the day, but could walk normally when it was dark. She wondered what the moon had to do with his ability to walk; it was a question she'd have to ask him sometime.

Kyra suddenly remembered that the boys were still outside. She turned and quickly opened the backdoor. At the bottom of the stairs were Bill and Aaron. Bill's, face was red and his breath was coming in short pants. He was struggling to pull Aaron, sitting in his wheelchair, up the short flight of stairs.

"A little help here?" Bill said grinning. "Aaron must have put on a few pounds since the last time I had to do this."

"I'm so sorry," Kyra apologized. "I forgot about the stairs!"

"Ya, most people do when they can walk," Aaron said. "I'm freezing out here."

Kyra and Bill pulled Aaron to the top of the stairs and tried to wheel him inside, but the wheelchair couldn't fit in the door. Kyra was embarrassed; thinking she should have known the wheelchair might not fit.

"Mom, get out here we have a problem!" She called.

The four adults got up from the table to see what help they could offer. Kyra heard Gustaf mumble under his breath, "I see the problem here."

Gustaf shimmied his slim body around Bill, the wheelchair and Kyra, reached down and picked Aaron up in his strong arms.

"Well what are you two waiting for? Fold it up and drag it in."

Kyra had no clue about how to fold up a wheel chair; it must have shown because Bill took charge and effortlessly folded the chair and dragged it into the house with Gustaf and Aaron following behind. Kyra stood there on the stoop, leaning against the railing, and watched through the door as Bill popped the chair back open and Gustaf unloaded Aaron into his seat.

"Kyra, get in here and close the door."

"Umm ya," she said, walking in and shutting the door quietly.

"Thanks Gustaf," Aaron said. "I thought for a moment I might turn into an *'Aaronsicle'*, before Bill and Kyra got me inside."

"I am so sorry!" Kyra exclaimed shamefully.

She walked over to Aaron and hugged him warmly, rubbing his arms and legs trying to get him warm again.

"You didn't know my wheelchair wouldn't fit through the door and it wasn't like you did it on purpose."

"Its something I should have thought about."

"Could you, uhm, hug me a little tighter please, oh ya. Um just a little longer. I think I am starting to get warm," he said chuckling.

Kyra pulled back like a snake had bitten her and stomped out of the kitchen to search for Andrea, Bob and Bobette.

She heard Aaron yell from the kitchen, "What did I do!"

If he thought that would get a response out of her he was sorely wrong. She went into the living room, grabbed a few pillows from the couch and handed some to Andrea; the two lay out on the carpeted floor and propped the pillows under them for added comfort. Bob and Bobette Bigfoot were jumping up and down on the couch. Kyra just got comfortable on the floor when Aaron, followed by Bill, rolled into the living room. He sat there for a moment looking around the room and then he broke out into a hearty laugh when he saw the Bigfoot leaping up and down on the couch; the springs groaning under their weight.

"That couch must have some heavy duty springs," Aaron said, laughing.

Then 'sprung' Bob sunk; his legs looking as if the couch had eaten them. Bobette reeled with laughter, howling, as she watched Bob trying to free himself from the broken couch. The rest of them could only watch in stunned silence as Sunny ran into the room, waving her finger and scolding Bob with her every step. It didn't take a rocket scientist to know the couch was toast. Sunny wrapped her arms around Bob's furry foot, twisted and pulled it free. Bob was so grateful he planted a big sloppy wet kiss on Sunny's cheek. Then he hugged her tightly in his long hairy arms; her face flushed red and her lips almost turned blue before he finally released her. Bobette stood watching with her hands on her hips fuming. She viewed Sunny as a competitor for her Bob's attention. She swooned when Bob turn and swept her in his arms, nuzzling her hairy neck softly with his nose, causing her to squirm and giggle.

"Ewwww" Aaron exclaimed.

The rest were too stunned yet to react.

"Well I think it's sweet," Sunny said, wiping drool from her face. She grimaced a little walking back into the kitchen.

Andrea and Kyra stuffed pillows down in the couch to fill the large holes and replaced the cushions. The two Bigfoot sat down snuggling in each other's arms, like two teenagers at a drive-in-movie. Bill who had been sitting quietly got out of his chair and offered it to Andrea, then gestured to the other chair for Kyra to sit down. Once the two girls were settled, Bill moved the coffee table against a wall to make a cozy spot for Aaron next to the Bigfoot. Aaron's protests went unnoticed as Bill forcibly rolled Aaron to his spot both sputtering and stammering in laughter trying to rebuke the others logic of the move. Finally with Aaron in place, Bill plopped himself down on the chilly floor. No one had noticed that Bob had the remote until he started flicking through channels. To add to the interesting flickers of scenes, Andrea uttered jokes and puns sending the rooms occupants into fits of giggles. Aaron and Bill not wanting to be bested joined in the game and soon there was not a dry eye in the living room. They laughed so hard they cried.

"Stop it," was all Kyra could say as she rolled off the chair onto the floor unable to stop laughing.

Bob found a show that captured his attention because the flickering stopped and they all watched an animated cartoon about a boy who changed into a dragon. Andrea's eyes sparkled and shined as she watched the boy dragon and wished she had a guy like him. It was dusk, when Sunny, Gustaf and Thaliana came into the living room to get Bob and Bobette to bring them back home to The Farm. Bob and Bobette did not want to go; they liked the sagging couch and enjoyed snuggling on it.

After much debating and pleading, Sunny decided to let the Bigfoot take the broken couch. They happily carried the couch out of the house and placed it in the back of the van. Sunny, Thaliana, and Gustaf took turns unconsciously checking the clock on the wall. Kyra and the rest stared at them like they were animated figures in a store window. They wondered what they were waiting for. They did not have to wait long. The doorbell rang and Sunny quickly answered the door. She was smiling as she ushered a scowling Noelle into the living room.

"We have another guest." Sunny announce. She quickly glancing at Kyra with her 'mined your manners' look. "She's spending the night."

Kyra, Aaron and Andrea turned and looked at Bill for answers; he only shrugged his shoulders looking as perplexed as they were. Kyra was stunned that her mother would be so blind as to bring one of her school tormentors to their home. Then she announced that Noelle was spending the night with all of them. Thaliana and Gustaf smiled at Noelle, by the look on their faces they were mind speaking to her, about what none of them knew, for Thaliana had a gift for blocking things she did not want known. Noelle stood there, her face softening a little; a smirk creased the side of her small mouth as she nodded and sat on the floor where the couch once rested.

"I suppose you all would like to know why she is here," Gustaf's rich voice boomed, knocking them out of their stupor.

Gustaf's told them that his daughter, the mother of Bill and Noelle, was an opal colored dragon named Nadia, who fell in love with a human man. Nadia, fearful that if her boyfriend knew she was a dragon might not want to marry her, had hidden it from him even after they were married. Their first born, William, was born out at the farm.

His father was kept busy at home during the birth, for how would Nadia explain their son hatching from and egg. Though Bill was born looking more like a dragon, the witches and wizards cast a protective spell so Bill could change into human form until he was able to do it himself. The whole dragon community was proud of have a 'Humragon' in their mist it was a rarity. Then when Nadia became pregnant with Noelle, she carried her like any human would and gave birth as a human. Noelle came out pink, sandy colored hair, large brown eyes and a perfect human baby. Out of precautions, Bill and Noelle's father was detained, until after the birth, once again on *The Farm*. Nadia soon discovered that even though Noelle was not really a 'Humragon' she was a 'Druman'. Drumans are shape shifters in one form or another; they may only be able to change into one or more shapes. The revelation occurred when Nadia discovered Noelle had disappeared when she was a toddler and a stray cat showed up in their house. The cat was dark as night, gleaming golden green eyes, and a tail long sleek and willowy that most other cats might envy if they knew what envy was. Nadia fed the cat and then she called her husband Chuck before calling the police. Chuck came home speedily from his job, worried lines creased his face as he too search desperately for Noelle all over the neighborhood; he had been still searching when the police came and questioned Nadia. Day had turned to a brisk cold damp night. Chuck wrapped his arms around his sobbing wife trying to offer her any comfort he could, masking his own fear. Bill was safely snoring in his bed with Thaliana watching over him, rocking quietly in the rocking chair in the corner of his room. She had come as soon as she heard Noelle was missing to help her grieving sister and brother in law.

Two more days went by, each of them feeding the stray cat, stroking it as it sat of there laps and purred. The cat roaming the house brought a certain comfort to all of them, only Bill seemed enthralled by the cat following it everywhere and calling it Oel. When night came and Bill was once again asleep in his bed, Chuck was by his side reading a children's story to him while Thaliana and Nadia sat in the living room wondering where Noelle could have gone; each silently praying for a miracle. In a blink of an eye their prayers were answered as Oel, the cat that Nadia had been stoking, transformed into Noelle the toddler. With tears of joy streaming down her face, Nadia wrapped Noelle in her loving arms. Thaliana joined her sister in happiness and rescued Noelle from her mothers squishing embrace.

Thaliana and Nadia came up with a quick explanation to tell Chuck. They would say that a strange woman found Noelle wondering around in the backyard, took her into her home and kept her for a few days. When she found out who the child belonged to she brought her home. They called frantically for Chuck. He almost injured himself sprinting into the living room to see what the matter was, his heart pounding with a mixture of fear and hope. When he saw Noelle wrapped in a blanket in Thaliana's arms a dam burst inside him somewhere, sending rivets of water from his eyes. He took his baby girl into his thick strong arms, tucking her head in his neck and wept. When he was finally able to speak again, Nadia told him, with red-rimmed eyes, the story they had concocted.

When Chuck asked whom the woman was Nadia told him that she really didn't know. That she and Thaliana were so happy to have Noelle they didn't get a chance to ask and that when they looked up she was gone.

Chuck asked Thaliana and Nadia a barrage of questions until the two of them were weary. They suggested Chuck called the authorities and inform them that Noelle had been found. Four hours later and many questions answered the police left their. Thaliana thought it wise to have a wizard cast a spell on Noelle so she could not change at will until she was older. When the spell was cast, all were relieved and things went back to normal.

Thaliana sighed when Gustaf finished his story; it sounded like a small feather of wind amongst the silence. They all sat or stood looking at him to make sure it was the end. A quick shadowy blur shot across the room, echoed a loud merrouw and flew in Kyra's direction. Gustaf's arm darted out and grabbed the shooting shadow by the scruff of the neck, while it squirmed and twisted in its grip.

"None of that," Gustaf said. "We are all friends here."

Noelle morphed back into human form; Gustaf was still gripping her neck firmly in his hand.

"I just wanted to sink my claws into her," she purred. "That's all grandpa." She was staring at Kyra all the while.

"That will be enough. No granddaughter of mine will behave in such a manner. I will not tolerate it!"

Gustaf let go of Noelle's neck and she skulked back to her place by the wall, stealing glances at Kyra like she could devour her. Kyra only smiled back. She now knew Noelle's secret and if she got out of line Kyra knew how to handle her. She had a cat cage in her closet from a previous cat they owned when she was younger. She giggled silently at the revelation that if she had to she could beat Noelle at her own game.

With some long goodbyes and many hugs and kisses all around Gustaf, Thaliana and the pair of Bigfoot finally took their leave. Grammy also said her goodbyes; she had some things of her own to do.

Kyra and her new friends sat and silently watched television, each lost in their own thoughts, while Sunny fixed them a snack tray of fruit. When she had finished she called them all into the kitchen to eat. Bill and Aaron hurried into the kitchen with Noelle following behind.

"Shall we?" Kyra gestured to Andrea with an outstretched arm towards the door.

"I think we shall," Andrea replied, with a cockney accent.

"Always a comedian," Noelle murmured loudly.

They all sat and greedily stuffed fruit into their mouths. Laughing at each other as the sweet juice dribbled down their chins. Kyra was happy to see Sunny join them. Her face beaming and her chin wet with the sweet juice. When the laughter ebbed and their stomachs were satisfied Sunny announced that it was time for them to go to bed. She also had to figure how to get another couch before her husband got home from his trip. And then there was the matter of Grackle. She thought long and hard of the plans Gustaf and Thaliana told her about him.

Sunny cleaned out the guest room where Aaron and Bill would sleep for the night. Andrea and Noelle would slumber with Kyra in her room.

"Goodnight," they all called to Sunny as they made their way up the stairs.

The girls walked into Kara's bedroom and Noelle eagerly pounced on Kyra's bed claiming it for her own.

"Let's not get into a cat fight ladies!" Andrea said.

She watched Kyra and Noelle staring each other down. Kyra's jaw was clenched in fury while Noelle jumped up from the bed and sauntered around her purring and hissing.

"I'll tell you what," Noelle compromised. "If you let me sleep at the foot of your bed in cat form I promise not to scratch your eyes out."

"It's a deal," Kyra agreed. "If you promise not to leave fleas on my sheets."

The two stared each other down with bad intentions. Andrea stepped in between the two, to ease the tension. About the same time Sunny walked into the room to drop off sleeping bags for Andrea and Noelle. When Sunny walked into the room Noelle quickly told her she didn't need a sleeping bag. She explained that Kyra and she had a deal. Sunny shrugged her shoulders and left; taking the sleeping bag with her.

"No funny stuff, right," Kyra asked Noelle.

She wanted to make sure their agreement was understood.

Noelle nodded, morphed into her cat form and settled herself at the foot of Kyra's bed. Andrea went to work unrolling her sleeping bag and Kyra quickly changed into her PJ's. Kyra offered Andrea a pair which she gladly accepted. The intrepid youngsters settled in for the night; safe from the wickedness of the world. But the night was short and none could have ever imagined the challenges they would face the following day.

Chapter 15
THE PHONE CALL

The five of them were up well before dawn, ate breakfast and then they all crowded onto Kyra's bed.

"I slept like a log," Bill said.

"Well you snore like a bear," Aaron added.

"That's nothing," Noelle put in. "Kyra talks in her sleep."

"You think that's bad," Andrea started to say, but she never got to finish her sentence. Sunny burst into the room. Her face was contorted and she was breathing raggedly. She stopped just inside the doorway, trying to catch her breath; her eyes darted from face to face as if she were trying to decide whom her sight should settle on. Then she took a deep breath and belted out frantically.

"He has your mother!" She cried, gravely.

Tears began to roll from her wide eyes. She stepped into the room, shaking her head as if she were trying to make sense of it all.

"Mom," Kyra asked, anxiously. "What are you talking about?"

She and Andrea quickly hurried by her side and helped her sit down on the bed. Sunny turned and looked at Bill and Noelle. She reached out blindly and took each by the hand.

"I am so sorry I have to be the one to tell you this. Grackle has your mother."

Bill and Noelle glanced at each other and then their eyes settled back on Sunny. They were hoping that she was mistaken somehow and that it had all been a bad dream, but the look on Sunny's face told them that this was no dream. The thought of their mother, her small framed body, dangling in Grackle's pointy talons flashed in their minds.

"What happened?" Noelle asked.

Sunny held their hands tighter as if it offered her some courage and comfort for Noelle and Bill. Nadia had been sitting in her kitchen when Grackle crashed through the roof of her house, grabbed her in his huge talons, squeezing her tightly in his grip and carried her off to his lair.

"Why didn't she just change—you know—into a dragon?" Bill stammered.

"I don't think she had a chance."

"What about our father?" Noelle asked.

"Fortunately he wasn't home."

Noelle and Bill sighed with relief; at least their father was safe from Grackles grasp. Their father would be devastated if he knew something had happen to his wife.

He loved her almost more than life itself; at least that's what he always told her. They imagined his reaction when he found out what had happed to his beautiful wife. They pictured him hurrying home and rummaging through the wreckage hoping somehow to find his wife buried underneath it unharmed. They wondered if his beautiful soft hazel green eyes were brimming with tears. Not knowing that she was abducted.

Chatter started to ensue among the group and Sunny quickly quieted them down.

"There's more," she said, staring at Andrea. "Your mother is missing too."

"No," Andrea said. No, you're lying."

"No, sweetheart. It's true."

"But how?"

"Gustaf thinks it was Grackle or his minions. When your mother found out about Nadia she called and told Gustaf. He then sought the council about the matter and immediately went to get your mother, but by the time he got there she was gone. Upon further inspection of her house he found scratch marks on the balcony. Gustaf is at *The Farm* as we speak and the council has already assembled. There're deciding on how to proceed next."

"What's the council going to do," Noelle asked. "Sit around and talk while that monster kills my mom!"

It was the final straw for her. Noelle broke down in tears, leaning towards her brother for support and comfort. Kyra put her arms around Andrea and hugged her tightly. Andrea stood rigid; her face was a mixture of confusion, anger and sadness.

"I'm not going to let him get away with this!" she said, pulling away from Kyra. She turned and stormed angrily out of the room.

Her sobs could be heard echoing off the tiled bathroom walls. The rest of them stood and waited silently for her to return. Andrea came back into the room; her eyes were hard, her jaw set, and her fists clench. Sunny understood her anger, her rage.

"Gustaf said the council will decide," Sunny said, evenly. "I'll—um—leave you for now. I want to call your father."

They all nodded except for Andrea; she stood cemented like a statue as Sunny left the room and closed the door.

"We have to do something," Andrea said when Sunny had left. "The council won't be able to decide on a course of action for days."

"Yeah," Bill said. She's right. The politics behind it all could take weeks."

They all jumped when someone rapped on Kyra's window. Andrea reached for her shoe and Kyra for her bat. Noelle held up her hand to stop them.

"It's a friend," she said, tranquilly. "I called her. She can help."

A face glowed through the window. She had thin lips and large oval blue eyes that shone like crystals.

"Shannon! Kyra said, surprised.

Noelle unlocked the window and let her in. Shannon jumped up and down warming herself from the cold night air.

"What is she doing here?" Kyra asked.

Bill, Andrea and Aaron were looking at Shannon as if they were primed to pounce on her. Noelle smiled reassuringly.

"I called her to help."

"How," Andrea asked, keeping a sharp eye on Shannon. "You didn't use the phone."

"Well you know that whole witch and black cat thing."

"Oh come on," Kyra asked. "You're not going to tell us she's a witch."

"Actually, I am," Shannon said, facing them with all the pride and confidence she could muster.

Kyra, Andrea, Bill and Aaron huddled together and talked out all the possibilities. Bill had no idea that Noelle's friend Shannon was a witch, but there were a lot of things he didn't know about his little sister. They all agreed it was possible. Andrea turned and stared into Shannon's crystal blue eyes.

"Well, any ideas witch?" She spat.

Shannon looked at all of them and smiled.

"I heard about your parents and I came up with this plan..."

Shannon's plan was simple; gear up, head to the north and attack Grackle on his own territory rather than fight him in the Duluth/Superior area. She would cast a spell of stealth, invisibility, with Noelle's help, and a spell to keep Kyra, Noelle and herself warm on the journey. She stopped abruptly when the window rattled, followed by a light crunching noise and a sound like a distant helicopter coming in through the window.

"Allow me," Andrea said as the others watched stunned.

She reached out and pulled a small ruby red dragon inside.

"Rachel!" Aaron, Bill and Noelle said in unison.

Rachel squirmed and wiggled out of Andrea's grip. Then she turned into a thin, skinny little girl, with stunning dark hazel eyes, auburn hair and a look of innocence that was almost believable, but under the circumstances they all knew it was a facade.

"I'm going too or I'm gonna tell!" Rachel said stamping her little foot hard on the floor.

She crossed her arms and stood firmly in place; there was a look of defiance and determination on her small face.

"Great!" Andrea muttered.

"Who is she?" Kyra asked, quite confused about what was transpiring.

"My little sister," Andrea replied. "Matthew's twin."

"You never told me."

"You never asked."

"We could tie her up" Bill quipped; with his usual humor, only this time it wasn't funny to anyone.

The group left the room to discuss Rachel's fate. They argued and talked until they finally came to a decision about her. Andrea sulked at the decision but the majority ruled and the majority said Rachel would come with them under the condition that she promised to obey them. Rachel was jumping for joy and dancing around the room like a ballerina. She had been listening at the door. She pledged her loyalty to the group the moment they walked into the room.

"Were you listening?" Andrea asked suspiciously.

Rachel beamed, her stunning eyes glowing, and then she vanished into thin air. The others stood staring at the spot where she had been standing stunned and silent. Then Bill suddenly felt a poke in his side.

"Hey?" Bill asked. "Why did you do that Andrea?"

"Do what," she replied.

"Poke me in the side."

"I didn't do anything."

"Well somebody did."

Then Kyra felt a poke in her side and then Andrea did too.

"It Rachel," Andrea said.

"But where is she?" Kyra asked.

Aaron finally figured it out. He waited until Rachel went around the room poking each one in turn and when she came around to him he reached out and grabbed hold of her arm. Rachel quickly materialized before their eyes and was squirming like a rat in a trap to get away.

"You never told me you could do that," Andrea said. "Does mother know?"

Rachel shook her head no vigorously.

"Well, don't do it again unless you absolutely have to."

"Let's get this show on the road!" Bill said.

The group agreed that Kyra and Shannon would decide what they needed since they were both human. Shannon might have been a witch and even witchy in attitude at school, but she was still a human. Kyra grabbed a couple empty worn backpacks from under her bed, while Shannon grabbed the supplies they would need from the kitchen downstairs. Kyra went through her drawers; she pulled out pairs of wool socks, two sets of long underwear, undergarments, four pairs of mittens and three sets of gloves. She found snow pants in her closet, winter jackets, which could withstand frigid temperature at 20 degrees below zero, and two pairs of insulated snow boots. Living in the Duluth/Superior area for so long gave Kyra the confidence that she knew how to pack for a trip up to the Arctic Circle. Aaron found a map of Canada in Kyra's dresser drawer; it was the same drawer where she kept her special undergarments. It made her blush; she wondered if Aaron had noticed. Shannon came back to the room with dozens of energy bars, twelve bottles of water, which were floating in the air behind her, five silver emergency blankets and a small first aid kit.

She and Kyra packed what they needed for the trip and dressed themselves for the freezing temperatures. When they were dressed, and looking a little bulky, Shannon reached into Kyra's closet and pulled out a few scarves.

"We're going to need these," she said, wrapping one around Kyra's face, leaving only her bright eyes showing. Then she wrapped one around her face.

Bill, Aaron, Andrea and Rachel wouldn't need to dress warmly for the trip. As long as they stayed in dragon form they would be fine. Shannon would also use her powers to cast a warming spell around them if needed and Noelle's fur, in her cat form, would keep her warm. They were ready for the long arduous journey, but they would wait until nightfall before setting out.

The day had passed quickly and night was upon them. They waited until they were sure Kyra's mother was asleep and then they set their plan in motion.

"Let's go." Andrea ordered.

Shannon and Kyra followed the others out the door, down the stairs and into the dark of the night. Aaron, Bill and Andrea morphed into dragons and Rachel followed suit. Kyra had wished in her heart she could say goodbye to her mom, Grammy and her father. She was concerned that she might not return. With that thought in mind, she climbed on Aaron's back. She could have sworn she heard her mother and Grammy's voice whispering, "Goodnight darling and good luck."

Chapter 16
IN THE DARK OF THE NIGHT

With Kyra riding Aaron's back, Noelle on Andrea, Shannon on Bill and Rachel flying beside them, her little wings flapping diligently, they took off silently into the dark of the night. The force of the wind bit into Kyra's skin and caused her eyes to water the higher they climbed. She flattened herself against Aaron's lithe body so that the wind would cascade gently around her. Then she glanced over to see how the others were doing. Shannon was also looking around; she was mouthing silent words and smiling. A wave of warmth washed over Kyra's chilled body and stung her eyes. Kyra smiled at Shannon knowing she had cast a spell that had warmed her.

Before they took flight Aaron told Kyra they could probably fly at 25 kilometers per hour, which was approximately 40 miles per hour. At that rate he figured they should rest every four hours, especially having Rachel along, since she would have to beat her wings faster to keep up with them.

In the darkness Kyra could see a twinkling of streetlamps and houselights as they flew. The ground was bursting with trees that looked like dark silhouettes, vehicles like rectangles and buildings like squares.

The further they flew; city blocks lined with buildings gave way to landscapes dotted with darkened trees that reached up towards them. The moon in the midnight sky came and went with the clouds. Once again she glanced over at the others to see how they were doing. Shannon was laying face down on Bill's back. Kyra could only guess she may have been sleeping; her eyes were closed and her face looked peaceful. Noelle was curled up in a ball, looking like a lump of coal on Andreas back; she too was most likely taking a catnap.

The sight made Kyra laughed with delight. She scanned the horizon for Andrea's little sister, Rachel, and her heart sputtered when she did not see her at first. Rachel was flying so close behind Aaron she seemed almost invisible. When Rachel saw Kyra looking at her she smiled a toothy grin and spoke to her in thought.

Boring isn't it.

Kyra nodded her head and thought back.

Yes, very boring indeed.

Kyra turned, facing forward once more, and yawned; she lay down and covered her face with her arms and fell softly to sleep.

Her mind spun with confusion when she found herself face to face with Grackle once again, only this time at her feet laid a pool of blood. Her eyes were darting, looking for the source. When she found it she gasped loudly in horror, for their laid Thaliana. Her side was sliced opened and her teeth were red, perhaps from Grackles blood. She looked back at Grackle and she notice pink bite marks on his whitish gray neck. He grinned at her and thought into her mind, you're next.

Kyra sat up screaming; she was scrambling to get away from her vision. She slipped, slid off Aaron's back and plummeted towards the tree filled ground below. Aaron and Rachel went into action. Rachel being the smaller and quicker of the two maneuvered in quickly and caught Kyra on her back. The extra weight knocked Rachel down another ten feet before she finally made a correction and flew to Aaron's side. Kyra clung to Rachel's small body shaking and self-conscious; she didn't want the others to know what she saw in her vision. The last thing any of them needed was more stress. Rachel glided down to the ground and landed and the rest followed. Kyra explained that she had fallen asleep and was startled when she woke and realized she was flying. She could tell by their faces they didn't really believe her, but what choice did they have. None could say she was a liar, not knowing themselves what really happen. The dragons each morphed back into human form and gave her caring hugs. Even Noelle and Shannon joined in to Kyra's amazement. They rested, ate and talked a little; lost in their own thoughts about what they were going to do once they reached Grackles lair. Shannon passed the water around and each in turn took a long drink before screwing the cap back on tightly.

They had talked earlier about conserving their water since it was the heaviest and most precious thing they carried. Bill announced, before they mounted up to fly, that he thought they were by Churchill, near Hudson Bay. Kyra had not spent very much time studying Canada; she found it difficult to comprehend where Bill said they were. Aaron noticed how confused Kyra looked and came to her rescue. He pulled out the map and pointed to where Bill said they might have been. Kyra smiled and gazed deeply into Aaron's brown eyes. She was blushing with the thought that the two of them might become sweethearts. Aaron tossed Kyra high into the air, to her delight, shifted into dragon form and she landed safely on his back. The others smiled and teased the two lovebirds. Rachel was the only one who seemed bewildered about the whole thing. She didn't have a clue what they were giggling about as they took flight into the brisk, moonless, sky.

Bill projected his thoughts to Shannon and Kyra. He told them that they did not fly through the clouds because it was much too wet. Then he took Shannon playfully through one to show her, but Shannon had been ready for his stunt. She cast a spell that kept her dry as a bone, but Bill came out glistening with water droplets. Kyra and the others laughed when they saw that Bill's plan had backfired. Bill laughed right along with them when he realized that Shannon had outdone him. Andrea and Kyra watched while Bill flew in circles and preformed fancy maneuvers trying to impress Shannon with his ability. *I think he likes her*, Kyra thought into Andrea's head. Andrea responded with a slight nod as she quickened her pace and knocked Bill with her tail. *Behave,* she told him with her mind, sending it out for all to hear. Shannon's face reddened and everyone knew it wasn't from the cold.

She liked Bill too and she knew he was showing off for her. The group descended lower, taking advantage of eddies caused by the wind. Kyra could see waves cresting. Hudson Bay in all its glory lay beneath them. The energy bar she had eaten earlier had her feeling sleepy again. She was afraid to sleep; afraid of having that dream about Grackle and Thaliana's bleeding body. She tried desperately to stave off sleep, but found it difficult, so she started singing to herself. Rachel flew close to Kyra and asked her why she was singing a children's rhyme. Kyra didn't realize it was the same rhyme from Aaron's note. She started singing a rock song and before she knew it, it turned into a nursery rhyme about Grackle. Frustrated she laid her head down on Aaron's glimmering scales and closed her eyes to think. Shannon had been watching and cast a spell of peaceful slumber on Kyra and she went fast to sleep.

In her dreams Kyra was walking hand in hand with Aaron along Lake Superior's shore. They stopped and Aaron asked her for a kiss. She giggled and blushed as their lips met again and again. It was so real to Kyra and she felt happy. For the first in her life she had found someone she really cared for; her heart pounded at every thought of him; his presence; his laugh; his manner, and then she woke, feeling warm and content. She had been kissing Aaron's back in her sleep.

Smoochie, smoochie, she heard the voice of Rachel giggling in her head. Then Rachel sang a chorus of: *Aaron and Kyra sitting in a tree, K-I-S-S-I-N-G.*

Kyra looked around at the others and they were all grinning.

"Enough all ready," she said. "I don't know what you're talking about."

"We do," the group chimed in unison.

They landed for the second time and Bill claimed they were close to the Melville Peninsula. *How does he know?* Kyra thought. Perhaps he had a built in GPS system somewhere in his golden dragon body. She started to wonder if the rest of them had the same uncanny ability as Bill, but felt too foolish to ask. She checked her watch; it was 3:20 am. They were making better time than she expected. Though they all knew the most difficult part of the journey was still to come; reaching Grackles lair unnoticed and in one piece. Kyra reached into the backpack and handed out the silver emergency blankets. She hoped that it would provide enough cover to help keep them warm. Shannon and Bill snuggled together in their blankets, taking sips of water and sharing an energy bar. Andrea and Noelle, still in cat form, curled up under Andrea's blanket and Aaron wrapped his around Kyra and himself.

Kyra's mind wandered over the days events that had bought them to this place so far from home. She wondered if her mother or Grammy knew they were missing; her heart filled with a longing of home. Though she had traveled much in her short life, her family had always been there and now she was with her friends. Aaron wrapped the blanket tightly around them and the two shared an energy bar. Rachel crawled into Andrea's blanket, almost squishing Noelle in the process, as she snuggled close to her sister for warmth. Kyra smiled at the two sisters; she wished her parents had had another child besides her. She was grateful for Andrea and the friendship they shared. Bill being as outspoken as ever asked Shannon why wasn't her spell of warmth working.

"I don't know," she said, through chattering teeth. "Maybe it ran out of fuel."

"It has to be Grackle." Aaron said, contemptuously.

Then all fell fast to sleep knowing that the next leg of their journey would be even more treacherous.

Chapter 17
THE LAST LEG

The intrepid group of youngsters settled in for the night. They all knew that the further North they traveled the colder, darker and more desolate the environment would become. Though they all had their doubts about being able to rest comfortably in the freezing cold, all were soon fast asleep; protected by Shannon's dream spell. During the course of the night Andrea was awaken by the sound of snow crunching under foot. She peeked through her blanket to see where the sound was coming from and laughed when she saw Aaron coming back from what she assumed was a potty run. He climbed underneath the silver blanket and wrapped Kyra tightly in his arms.

They slept peacefully through the night, but they were shocked out of their dreams by a hideous laughter that seemed to echo through the still darken landscape. Bill was on his feet quickly pulling Shannon to hers. The rest of the group stumbled groggily and tried to find their bearings. They began stuffing blankets into the backpacks and gearing up to take flight.

"Where on earth did that sound come from and who made it?" Andrea asked.

"I don't know," Bill replied. "But I got the strangest feeling that we're being watched."

"It was probably one of Grackle's minions," Aaron said. "It's a sure bet he knows we're coming." Then he turned to Kyra and asked, "What time is it?"

"It's 8:00am. But why is it still dark.

Bill stepped up and answered her question.

"The further north we fly the difference in the tilt of the earth determines the night season and the daylight season. Night can last up to six months."

"That explains why I can still walk," Aaron said.

Kyra looked at Aaron standing tall and smiled brightly. Their eyes met and a feeling of euphoria swept over them both. It was then the dream that Kyra had longed to become a reality came true. Aaron kissed her gently on the lips. It was a sweet, endearing, kiss. They stood there wrapped in each other's arms; lost for a moment in a world that belonged only to them.

"All right you two," Bill called loudly. "Break it up!"

"Time to fly," Andrea said, lightheartedly softening Bill's interruption.

They took flight into the indigo sky. Andrea knew it wasn't a secret that Aaron and Kyra would soon be an item, but she had a secret of her own.

Andrea's thoughts were filled with love for a man she could never have. Unknown to Kyra, Andrea had a secret crush on her father years ago, but it soon waned. He was married to Sunny, but she still admired him. She knew she was much too young a dragon for a mate, but her heart still skipped a beat when she thought about him. He was so straight laced she would always have to hide her dragon side from him. She thought of Sunny's life and in her heart of hearts grieved for her. She knew that it was hard being lonely, but it was much worse being with someone and still feeling lonely and for that she did not envy Sunny at all.

Bill announced, as they flew, that they were now over the Summerset Island just off Baffin Bay. The landscape was a stunning sight. Kyra thought if it hadn't been so cold perhaps she could have stayed there forever; lost in its pristine beauty. Shannon and Kyra trembled in the cold, blistering, wind. Aaron and his dragon clan seemed totally oblivious to it. Aaron, being in tune with Kyra's bio rhythms, sensed her discomfort and released a burst of radiating heat from his body.

Better? He thought into her mind.

Yes much. Thank you. She replied.

She glanced over her shoulder to see how Shannon was doing and realized that she and Bill were having the same conversation. Rachel was keeping up with them swimmingly; the long track through the cold didn't seem to bother her at all. She did loops, every now and again, to stave off her boredom and to show off her acrobatic skills. The heat radiating from Aaron and the thought of how wonderful it felt to be kissed by him lulled her into a peaceful sleep. There were no dreams this time only the gentle rocking of Aaron's body under hers.

Kyra, Bills voice echoed in her head.

Huh, she sleepily thought back.

We're at Ellesmere Island now. You'll have to wake up soon.

Okay mom, just ten more minutes, she replied and then she drifted back to sleep embraced by the warmth and safety she felt being close to Aaron.

The sky was pitch black as they made their way, guided by some internal sonar, to just outside of Grackles lair. When they had landed Shannon laid down a protective spell of stealth and invisibility around them.

"Servo quod velieris nos ex suum spies," she chanted.

The spell translated from Latin was, *protect and hide us from the spies.*

She was hoping her spell would keep them safe while they scouted the area and devised a better plan. The spell she cast muffed any sounds or noises they made and gave them the ability to blend in and avoid detection from Grackle's centuries searching for intruders. Aaron gently slid Kyra down off his back while the others caught her and wrapped her in blankets to help shield her from the numbing cold. They were an unlikely group of warriors in a barren, icy landscape; four dragons, a witch, a cat and a human. As far as any of them knew, only dragons had ever set foot on this icy land; with the possible exception of the Inuit people. The dragons took turns changing into human form to eat, while the rest blew pulses of heat from their nostrils to keep the others from freezing. While Aaron ate he kept a watchful eye on Kyra as she slept; with every breath she took frosty puffs of vapor billowed from her mouth.

He was thankful that they had brought Shannon along. Without her spell of warmth Kyra's lungs would have frozen solid from the freezing cold. He grinned when he noticed what a cute couple Bill and Shannon made. Kyra hadn't really been sleeping; she was peeking through her eyelids at Aaron. She heard him telling the others about scouting around to locate Grackle's cave. Her heart sank at the thought that if he were detected and captured she may never see him again. She was afraid of losing him before she got the chance to really know him better. Then, almost as if she had read her thoughts, Andrea volunteered to do the exploring, locate Grackles cave and scout out how many followers he really had. Before she left she entrusted Rachel's care to Bill, Noelle, and Aaron.

"She's your cousin," she reminded them before she walked off into the darkness. "You be sure to take good care of her."

The moon was barely a sliver in the navy blue sky. The stars were almost suffocating and no matter where they looked their eyes were infused with their twinkling. Kyra looked up at the stars, closed her eyes and thought of the nursery rhyme, *Twinkle, Twinkle Little Star*. She allowed the words and melody to flow freely through her head. It gave her comfort and it helped her to dissipate any anxiety she was experiencing. They all sat and waited patiently for Andrea's return. She had been gone for about an hour. Rachel got up and started pacing back and forth across the ice. She was starting to worry about her big sister and so were the others, but they never let on.

"Andrea has been gone a long time," she whispered. "Do you think she's been captured?"

"I'm sure she's fine," Kyra said in an effort to comfort her.

"Yeah," Aaron added. "Andrea's smart enough to avoid being captured."

"You think so?" Rachel asked.

Everyone in the group nodded in agreement. In that same instance the sound of crackling ice and snow crunching under foot permeated the icy air. Someone or something was clearly making its way towards them. They held their breaths and stared into the darkness. When Andrea emerged from the icy miasma, Rachel jumped up and ran to her with outstretched arms.

"I was worried about you," she lovingly said to her big sister.

Then she took Andrea's hand in hers and led her back to the group. Andrea was weary and worn. She sat and replenished herself with an energy bar and a half bottle of water while the others waited patiently for her to give them a report. She ate her meager meal slowly as if it was going to be her last. When she had taken her final bite and drained the bottle of its contents she looked at the group gravely and spoke in a solemn tone.

"Grackle's lair is about thirty clicks from were we are positioned," she said, pointing to an outcrop of ice in the distance. "There's an icy cave off to one side and the main nest is higher up on a plateau over looking the ocean. It's impossible for anyone to reach on foot; flying is the only way to get in and out."

"How many of them are there?" Aaron asked.

"Their numbers are not as great as the Counsel might have thought. I counted around twenty or more, but I can't really be sure. It was rather difficult to tell from a distance."

Andrea's description of Grackle's lair gave Kyra a feeling of deja vu. It was exactly like her dream.

Bill stood up and looked deeply into Andrea's eyes. She knew what he was thinking even before he opened his mouth to speak.

"No," she said, staring back at him intently. "I didn't see your mom or mine. I had to stay hidden to avoid detection."

Bill bit his lower lip and bowed his head. Shannon came to his side and put her arm around his shoulder. Noelle strolled over and rubbed up against his leg. When Rachel started to cry Kyra went to her side and offered her comfort. The thought of losing her mom was more than her little heart could bear. Andrea held back her tears; she had to stay strong for her baby sister. Aaron walked up to Andrea and stood closely by her side.

"Do you think we can take them?"

Andrea looked into his cream colored face and conveyed what she knew to be the truth.

"We have a better chance of beating the *Devil in Hades*," she said.

"Than all is loss," Aaron whispered.

"What do you suggest we do?"

"We rest here for a while, gear up in a few hours and fly back home for reinforcements. I don't want to risk loosing any of you in a battle with Grackle."

The group settled down to reenergize for the long flight homeward; it was wiser to run and live to fight another day.

Chapter 18
SURPRISE

Rrrroar...! Reverberated off the glaciers; it was a sound deep and deafening. Large pieces of ice broke off from the top of the cavern and hurtled downward towards the frosty precipices below. The unlikely group were awaken from their slumber frighten and confused; their eyes darted around in the darkness, trying desperately to locate the source of the frightening sound. In their minds they knew it was Grackle. He had sensed their presence and sent out a small group of his most fierce minions to locate them.

"Get up everybody!" Aaron shouted. "We have to get moving fast."

The group quickly gathered up what they could and made ready to take flight, but it was too late. Three large, ferocious, dragons were descending upon them. Aaron quickly morphed into dragon form with Andrea and Rachel doing the same. Aaron grabbed Kyra and tossed her onto his back, Shannon and Noelle climbed aboard Andrea's and they took flight. Bill was still in human form, standing as still as a statue, looking up at the three mighty dragons as they made there descent.

"Bill!" Aaron shouted at him. "What are you doing? We have to get out of here!"

"It's too late Aaron," Bill answered. "We'll never make it. Take them and go. I'll handle these three."

The group watched from above as Bill quickly morphed into dragon form and let go of a mighty roar! Flames issued from his mouth and the sharp smell of sulfur permeated the frosty air. He took flight, angling straight for the three mighty dragons, flying in formation, growling and belching flames. Bill flew straight through the three dragons, breaking their formation. The group hovered above and watched as Bill turned and attacked a gray dragon twice his size, but what Bill lacked in size he made up for with speed. He swooped down, twisted his agile body and grasped the gray dragon's neck in his powerful jaws. He bit down hard and ripped a huge chunk from its neck. The large gray dragon roared in pain and fell like a stone to the icy chasm below. Shannon shrieked in terror when Bill was attacked from behind by the other two dragons. One was the color of crimson and the other was as black as coal. The crimson colored dragon caught Bill off guard; grabbing him from behind in its huge talons. The charcoal colored dragon flew in and raked its sharp claws deep into Bills underbelly.

"No!" Kyra screamed, but her cry was washed away with the wind.

Bill struggled to right himself as the dark dragon slashed relentlessly into his flesh. Blood oozed from the open wound and froze like icicles on the icy floor below.

"We have to help him!" Shannon screamed.

She uttered a spell in an attempt to protect him.

"Solvo him everto , permissum him vado. Vel I'll iacio vos tenus depths subter supter."

The spell translated was: *Release him demon, let him go. Or I'll cast you down to the depths below.*

The crimson dragon released Bill and turned his attention towards Andrea. Bill fell to the icy ground like a wounded dove.

Hang on; Aaron thought into Kyra's mind. He pulled his wings back tightly and flew straight at the charcoal colored dragon. Kyra could only watch in terror and hang on for dear life. The black dragon swung around to meet Aaron head on. Its chest inflated like a balloon as it sucked in the icy air and then *whoosh*—it released a stream of flames from its mouth like a blow torch. Instinctively, Kyra held up her hands in an attempt to shield her face from the flames. Miraculously her hands began to glow. A shimmering rainbow of light leapt from her hands and repelled the flames. The charcoal colored dragon took another deep breath, but before it got a chance to release its fury a blinding, pulsating, ray of white light radiated from Kyra's hands and struck the charcoal colored dragon directly in the eyes. The coal black dragon's whole body began to illuminate like the light from the sun. Its eyes suddenly dimmed and his massive frame fell from the sky like a stone; its body melted and disappeared into the icy ground below.

How did you do that? Aaron thought into Kyra's mind.

Kyra was as stunned as Aaron. She was looking at her hands in awe, but she didn't have time to try and figure out what happened. The crimson dragon was in pursuit of Andrea, Shannon and Noelle.

"Help!" Shannon cried.

Andrea was flying as fast as she could with the crimson dragon in hot pursuit.

"We're coming!" Aaron shouted.

With three flaps of his mighty wings Aaron was on the crimson dragon's tail. The crimson dragon sensing Aaron's present turned and snapped at him with its powerful jaws. Aaron rolled left, flew straight upward, flipped in mid air and flew straight at the crimson dragon.

Kyra, he thought into her mind. *Use your power.*

Okay, she thought back. *I'll try*!

She held up her hands and again a beam of white light radiated from them and struck the crimson dragon. The light was so intense that it pierced the blood red dragon and sliced it in two.

"Whoa," Aaron said, under his breath.

Andrea flew to Bill, lying on the icy floor, to offer him aid. Before she even reached him Shannon leaped off her back, in mid air, ran fervently to Bill and attended to his wounds. Bill was lying on his side; he was conscious, but his breathing was shallow.

"Hold still Bill," Shannon cautioned. Then she began to chant a healing spell.

She was able to undo some of the damage the gray dragon had inflicted, but some scars remained. Andrea and Aaron were able to move Bill to a nearby ridge so he could rest.

If Bill had been in human form he would have died from his injuries. Even as a dragon he was lucky to be alive. While he rested, with Shannon by his side, Aaron took a head count and found that Rachel was missing. He went to Andrea and asked if she had seen her. Andrea smiled.

"She's right here. Aren't you Rachel?"

Like magic Rachel appeared smiling.

"Is it over," she asked, looking wide eyed.

"Yes, it's over Rachel," Andrea answered.

"Are you angry at me for disappearing?"

Andrea grabbed her little sister and hugged her tightly.

"No honey. I'm not angry. You did the right thing this time."

While they talked Aaron went to check on Bill. He wanted to see if Bill was in any condition to fly.

"How you doin' Bill old bean?" Aaron asked his blood relative.

"I've been better."

"That was a pretty dumb thing to do. Go up against three adult dragons. You could have been killed."

"Yeah, I know, but they might have killed us all if I hadn't."

Aaron Smiled.

"I'm just glad you're okay."

Andrea was standing by Kyra's side staring at her in awe. She was wondering how Kyra created the rainbow of light that defeated the team of dragons. Kyra didn't have an answer for what had transpired. It was a mystery to her too.

"How did you do that?" Andrea asked.

Kyra shook her head.

"I don't know," she replied. "It just sort of happened."

"Well, let's just hope you can do it again when the time comes."

The group formed a circle around Bill; using their tails to create a mini-fortress.

"Now that Grackle knows we're here." Aaron said solemnly. "We have to confront him on is own ground."

The rest of the group grunted in agreement. Even Bill nodded knowing he would have to be left behind. The wind grew in velocity as if sending them a message to blow home and forget about the whole thing. Above the howling wind a new sound resurfaced; it was the sound of a thunderous roar off in the distance.

"You'll be safe here Bill," Aaron said. "Just keep out of sight and we'll come back for you when we can."

As the group made ready to go and face Grackle, Shannon had a change of heart.

"I can't leave him," she said.

"We know," Andrea offered.

The group bid Shannon and Bill farewell and reassured them they would be back as soon as they could. A sense of dread and foreboding cast an ominous shadow over them as they turned to leave Bill and Shannon in the chilling cold and the night that never ended. Even the moon had abandoned them.

"Let's go," Aaron said, glancing back at Bill and Shannon huddling together.

Five, of what had started out as seven, rose into the treacherous crisp air currents, shielding themselves for what laid ahead. *Grackle the terrible.*

Chapter 19
ALL IN A HARD NIGHTS WORK

Andrea led them to the spot where she had first spied on Grackle. It was a narrow precipice with an even narrower ledge just above Grackle and his followers. Around them fishers in the glacial surface creaked and groaned under their added weight.

"I hope this holds," Aaron said, as a small outcrop of ice broke off and shattered below.

From their vantage point, they could see the shadowy outlines of the cave, where a small flicker of light emitted from within, cast a dim glow on the dark figures of the dragons held captive inside.

"What do we do now?" Rachel asked. Her voice quivering in the realism of it all and the realization that this was no child's game they were playing.

"We wait," Andrea said, bravely. "I want to know where Grackle is before we go down there to try and find our mother."

The wind whipped at them relentlessly; it was a freezing, teeth chattering, wind, but they remained astutely vigil in their watch. They were so vigil that no one noticed when Rachel snuck off into the abysmal dark haze. Kyra shifted her, cold, stiff body, leaning in closer to Aaron for warmth. His broad body worked as a shield against the bitter wind. Northern lights flickering in the distant horizon caught her attention. The pristine beauty of their dancing glow mesmerized her. Her mind was lost in the warmth of its colors until it dimmed and faded into nothingness. Kyra fixed her eyes on Grackle's lair and noticed a shadow moving just outside the cavern. It appeared to be the form of a small dragon on the oblique landscape. The small dragon like form was gliding closer and closer towards the caves entrance. She watched the small form lean over and quickly peeked inside the cavern. The dim light form the cave cast a reddish glow on the dragons skulking outside. Then like magic the small form disappeared from view. Kyra continued to look on and noticed an enormous dragon step out beyond the cave door. Its mouth was open wide enough for her to see its sharp long spiked teeth gleaming red in the muted light.

Kyra didn't know much about dragons, but from her observation she guessed, by the way it walked and carried itself, it was a male dragon. He reached out his long, gnarled, spiky clawed hands and swiped the side of the cave where the small dragon had been crouching moments before.

Kyra gasped in horror when she saw he was holding a small red dragon tightly in his grip. Then she realized that the red dragon was Rachel. The large male held his prize high over his head, swinging it back and forth. The only thing Rachel could do was submit to his iron hold. The huge male called out in an earth shattering voice, "Look, I found a snack."

Andrea heard the commotion, reared up on her hind legs and roared fiercely in defiance. She jumped, in a spectacular leap, off the cliff and headed straight for Grackle. The enormous dragon, hearing Andrea's cry, raised his head and laughed. Andrea's passionate fury was fueled with whimsical malice.

"Grackle," she hissed. "Your mine!"

"How absurd," he bellowed, dangling Rachel in the air like a rag doll.

Kyra stood rooted in place; her mouth chastened in terror and her spirit pumped ferociously to keep her icy mind flowing. She was hoping that Andrea would veer away and break off her attack, but Andrea attacked Grackle head on. The shear size of Grackle gave the appearance of a mouse attacking a lion. She flew at him, fiercely blowing violet flames, but it was to no effect. He merely held up a hand and swatted them away. Using her tail she swiped at his coal black eyes, causing him to drop Rachel when he held up his claws in defense. Andrea swooped down trying to catch her sister, Grackle lashed out at her with his tail. His massive tail connected and sent Andrea soaring through the air. Rachel's angled form lay limp at Grackles feet.

"Kyra, Noelle," Aaron yelled. "Let's move. We have to go."

"No," Kyra cried. "We can't just leave Rachel behind."

"Now!" Aaron demanded.

Kyra and Noelle leaped onto Aaron's back just as the ice crumpled beneath them.

Aaron flew towards the spot they last saw Andrea cascading through the frosty air and Grackle was in hot pursuit. Aaron tried desperately to shake him; flying in and out of the hilly terrain of snow and ice.

"Down there!" Noelle purred, pointing to a fissure in the ice.

It looked just large enough for them, but too narrow for Grackle. Aaron flew towards the opening with Grackle trailing behind him, snapping at his tail. The fissure was barely big enough for them to fit through, but as they swooped lower it almost seem to widen. Without a second to spear Aaron flew into the crevice; ice rained down on them from above as Grackle slammed into the opening.

"We're going to be buried alive!" Kyra cried.

Chunks of ice rained down upon them. Aaron flew with the agility of an ace fighter pilot, avoiding large lumps of ice. Without warning Aaron looped around and headed back the way they came in.

"What are you doing?" Kyra shouted.

"We reached the end of the line," Aaron yelled. "We have to go back the way we came."

"But Grackle's out there."

"I know. That's just the chance we have to take."

Noelle and Kyra looked back and saw a wall of ice looming up behind them. It was then they understood Aaron's decision to turn around. Aaron reached the opening of the fissure and flew like a shot, up into the blackened sky. He was heading towards the only dim light visible. Grackle's lair.

"We'll have to find Andrea later," Aaron said.

"What about Rachel?" Kyra asked.

"Set me down on the cave floor," Noelle said. "I'll cat around and see what I can find."

When the cave came into view, they were shocked by what they saw. Clusters of dragons, all different colors and sizes were battling below. The place where Rachel had laid was now empty. The three of them looked around to see if they could locate her. They saw, among the tide of the dragons that fought and fell, Gustaf fighting side by side with a pewter dragon.

"Aiiii..!" Kyra screamed, as monstrous talons dropped out of the sky, engulfing her and Aaron in its grip.

Noelle managed to jump from Aaron's back just in time, landing safely on her cat feet on the ground below. The large dragon squeezed them tighter and tighter in its clawed talons, threatening to crush them in their grasp. Aaron tried to break free, but only succeeded in making their capture chuckle with amusement.

"Did you really think you were a match for me human?" Grackle chortled.

Kyra opened her mouth to scream, but the taste of warm, sticky, blood prevented her from doing so. Suddenly and inexplicitly they heard Grackle roar out in pain; he lost his grip on Kyra and Aaron and the pair fell like a rock towards the cave floor.

"My eyes! My eyes!" Grackle screamed.

"I'm tougher than I look," Noelle the cat said.

Aaron and Kyra screamed as they plummeted towards the icy, unforgiving, ground below. It would have most certainly been their death, had they hit the bone crushing ground, but a pair of sharp talons reached out and grabbed them in mid air. Only this time the talons that held them in its grasp were gentle and loving.

"Are you two all right?" a pewter dragon called to them from above.

It was Gunter, Andrea and Rachel's father.

Kyra smiled; she was happy that Andrea would have her father at last. Gunter carefully sat them on the ground and landed beside them. The fighting was sporadic as a few of Grackles minions fought to the death. A stunned silence filled Kyra as she watch two women wielding Excalibur swords; the women fought expertly and defended themselves against many attackers. The two women swung their swords with great agility and easily defeated their enemies. Kyra swayed when she realized the two women were her mother and Grammy.

A ruckus above her caused her to look up sharply into the night sky. Her gaze fell upon two silhouettes battling and slashing in furious combat. It was Grackle and Gustaf. Warm moist droplets pelted her face as she looked upward. It's raining, she thought, wiping her face. When she looked at her hands, however, what she perceived to be rain was blood raining down from above.

"Run...!" Aaron shouted.

He grabbed Kyra and pulled her out of the way just in time. Grackle and Gustaf plunged from the sky and crashed to the icy floor below. The ground shook and cracked from the impact. The two massive dragons twisted and turned ripping huge chunks of flesh from each other with each bite. Kyra's eyes brimmed with frozen tears as she watched the icy snowy ground turn from white to blood red. Grackle's opal Amulet was healing his wounds almost as fast as Gustaf could inflict them. Kyra pulled away from Aaron's grip and fled. She was focusing on thing and one thing only; defeat Grackle once and for all.

She approached the two dragons, locked in battle, and leaped onto Grackles back. Missing Gustaf's whipping tail by mere inches. She pulled herself along, using her legs for leverage. She slipped a little each time Grackle reached out and attacked Gustaf. Kyra held onto Grackle's scale with one hand, pushed up with her feet and then she flung herself forward. Her hands locked around the opal Amulet. She held onto the pendent with both hands and slid down the side of Grackle's body, but the Amulet didn't break as she had expected it to. She was dangling in the air holding onto the Amulet when without warning, her hands began to glow. Rays of rainbow light began to swirl around the Amulet The necklace broke sending her falling to the cold hard ground, but that was her least of her troubles because the two dragons, still locked in a death grip, threatened to crush her under their massive weight. Kyra got to her feet and tried to outrun their rolling bulk and suddenly felt herself hoisted in the air. Aaron had swooped down and saved her. Without his opal Amulet Grackle was defenseless. Gustaf roared and plunged his pointed fangs deep into Grackles neck.

"As the sun rises," Grackle said, glaring menacingly at Kyra. "So will your death."

His large black eyes dimmed and his body turned to dust. An eerie silence followed with the echo of shifting and crashing glaciers. Kyra turned and looked around. On the icy floor, once beautiful and pristine, lay dozens of broken and dying dragons. Beneath them darkened pools of blood. Tears rained from Kyra's eyes. The sight of the fallen was more than she could bear.

"Rachel?" she whispered.

"In there," Gunter pointed.

Aaron reached out, took Kyra by the hand and gently guided her into the cave. The cave glowed in a soft light emitted by thousands of jewels upon the walls. Sunny and her Grammy led them silently through huge passageways until they reached a small alcove off to the side. They entered in silence listening to the chatter of Rachel telling someone how brave she was. Looking up from her stupor, Thaliana sat clutching Rachel in her arms. Beside them Bill laid sleeping with Shannon and Nadia close by his side. Kyra smiled, almost laughing as a sense of relief washed over her; her friends were safe.

Chapter 20
THE CAVE OF SORROWS

The cave was littered with the bones of dragons, long dead and gone, piled up into heaping masses and fused into the icy walls like a crystal barrier. There were so many of them it was difficult to tell were the original path of bones began or ended. Aaron seemed mesmerized by them. He walked around the small alcove, with Kyra following close by his side, touching each one as he passed; it was if he could recognize whom the bones had belonged to.

"What are you doing?" Kyra asked.

"I thought maybe, just maybe, my parents might be among them," he replied, solemnly.

Kyra squeezed his hand tightly and he turned to look at her; his eyes were filled with pain and sorrow.

"Maybe Gunter would know?" Kyra said. "He's been here a for a very log time?"

Aaron nodded; then he turned his attention back to the icy bones once more and continued the process.

"Can I help?" Kyra asked.

This time it was Aaron who squeezed Kyra's hand.

"Are you sure you're up to the task?" He said, looking at her intently.

"I think so," she replied.

Together they navigated their way through the caverns of the cave. All around them the ice was speckled with reminders of the caves gory history and its newfound residents. The wizards and witches were scurrying around from dragon to dragon administering drinks, healing herbs and chanting spells of healing and rejuvenation. Aaron and Kyra were careful not to disturb them from their undertakings. When the two reached the front of the cave, Kyra spotted a gleaming object that lay just beyond the entrance. She walked briskly towards the object and realized it was the Opal Amulet. Kyra reached down, picked up the Amulet and offered it to Aaron.

"Here," she said, handing the Amulet to him. "This belongs to you."

"No, not me," Aaron said, taking a step back. There was a hint of fear in his caramel colored eyes.

"What's wrong?"

"The Amulet is evil. Can't you sense that?"

"No. I can't. Perhaps only dragons can sense its evil."

"Just put it away until we get a chance to ask Gustaf about it."

Kyra put the glowing Amulet in her jacket pocket, turned towards Aaron and rested her head on his chest. Than she lifted her head coyly and gazed into his beautiful, warm, brown eyes.

"Better?" she asked.

"Yes, thank you," he replied.

Aaron bent down and brushed his lips softly against hers.

"We better go."

"Yes. I think we better."

Aaron guided her back to the cave with his hand in the small of her back.

"Aaron, Kyra," Sunny called, her worried voice echoing off the cavern walls. "We've been looking all over the place for you. You must come—now!"

They looked at each other and then they peered at Sunny. She was all ready heading off into the distance at a quick pace. They caught up with her, out of breath and panting, to yet another alcove. In the dim light they could see Nadia, Rachel Bill, Andrea, Noelle, Gunter and Thaliana kneeling at the side of a large dragon. Wizards and witches were working eagerly around the huge frame, trying to heal its wounds. Aaron and Kyra stood transfixed, afraid of knowing why they had been summoned.

"Come on," Sunny said, snapping them out of their trance. "There isn't much time. He wants to see you two now."

They followed Sunny through the crowd of on lookers and their eyes settled on the face of Gustaf. He was lying on the cold ground badly wounded and dying.

"I waited for the two of you." Gustaf spoke, his tranquil voice filling their ears. "I wanted to say that I am proud of you both and that I love you very much."

Gustaf closed his eyes; his breathing was shallow and sparse and then his head slumped off to the side.

"It is finished," Thaliana said, lovingly touching her fathers arm.

Kyra's mind was swimming. She had all ready lost her real grandfather and the thought to losing Gustaf was too much for her to stand. She reached into her pocket and thrust the Amulet towards Thaliana.

"He doesn't have to die," Kyra screamed. "I have the Opal Amulet—please—please, see if it can save…"

Before she could finish she was whisked away sobbing, screaming and fighting to break free.

"It can save him," she moaned.

"Hush Kyra, hush," her mother said. "You know he wouldn't want that. His time has come."

Kyra quickly clamed herself and nodded. She knew her mother was right. Sunny and Grammy held her in their embrace and rocked her softly and slowly. The three of them sat on the icy ground and wept. They wept out of weariness. They wept out of the emptiness of loss. They wept out of relief that it was over. The others joined them when they were done giving their last respect to Gustaf. Kyra got stiffly to her feet and went to Gustaf's side. She stood on the tip of her toes, leaned over and kissed him on his cheek. Tears flowed from her eyes; she had loved him like her own Grandfather. She reached into her pocket, pulled out the amulet and murmured softly in his ear.

"This is for you," she said.

She reached out her hand towards Gustaf's cooling body and a beam of light emanated from the Amulet filling the entire cavern, and all the alcoves, in a radiant rainbow of light. Kyra was glowing with the continence of the sun.

Everyone turned away from Kyra; the light emitting from her was blinding. Their hearts pounded in mortification of what they thought she was doing. All they could do was stand and watch. A loud crack, like the shattering of a thousand windows, echoed through the light and it slowly faded away. Everyone in the cavern had to blink their eyes several times; it was like a hundred flash bulbs had gone off at the same time. Kyra stood there crying and shaking copiously; knowing she had done what she was supposed to do. Gentle arms wrapped around her and a warm voice whispered in her ear.

"Well done child. Well done."

Thaliana led her back to the group; the two of them sat and waited until everyone's vision had adjusted to normal.

"What happened?" Aaron asked.

"The right thing." Thaliana's voice boomed with pride. "The right thing."

Aaron went to her and held her hand. He smiled and his golden brown eyes danced with delight.

"Come on," he beckoned to her in a whisper. "There's something I want you to see."

He led Kyra out of the alcove and down the corridors until they reached the caves entrance. Kyra looked up into the glistening night sky that was filled with swirls of colors. Dragons in flight were silhouetted in its gleam. She stood awe struck by the sight, as the dragons seemed to dance along the beams. Weaving in and out, up and down, twisting and turning. A song reverberated through the night; it was the song of hope. Soon the others joined them at the cave entrance. Kyra watched as Aaron and the others took flight to join their dragon friends in their dance of light. They laughed when they saw Noelle, in her cat form, waving at them on Nadia's back before flying off.

Kyra's heart felt like it might burst from the splendor of the magnificent sight. Her heart radiated with hope and she knew that every living thing on the planet had somehow benefited from what had transpired. One by one the dragons flew back down and landed ready to take on a rider; it was time to go home; home where the heart is. Home to where the dragons soared above Lake Superior in the night sky. The Twin Ports area their stomping ground.

Chapter 21
HOME IS WHERE

The trip home was long and arduous. The wind whipped at them. Pulling at their clothes and causing the dragons to fly lower than they were accustomed too. Kyra, riding atop Aaron's back, smiled inwardly knowing that this was not the end of their time together. Before they left, Aaron had asked her to be his steady. She had stared into his big brown eyes, her blood coursing through her veins; she was putty in his hands. With a swift and loud "yes" the deed was done. They were a couple. She was his girl and he her beau. She glanced over to see how Grammy was doing riding atop Gunter's back. She seemed to be having the time of her life.

"Yoo-hoo!" Grammy called to Kyra. Her face beamed with happiness. It was obvious she was enjoying the ride home. The farther south they flew the longer the daylight lasted. Kyra wondered if Aaron would still be able to walk when they reached home. She wondered if the North Pole and its magnetic pull had something to do with it or perhaps it was the moon. It really didn't matter to her whether Aaron could walk or not because she liked him. In a wheelchair or walking he was still Aaron to her.

They stopped and rested a couple of times on the way home. The dragons changed into their human form to eat and drink. After a few hours, they loaded up again and took flight, eager to reach home. Kyra was worried, as they flew over Lake Superior that ships sailing in the lake might spot them along the way, but the others seemed unconcerned. The group flew over many ships along the way. Sometimes so close that Kyra felt she could have reached down and touched them.

Feeling sleepy from her adventure Kyra decided to lay back and just enjoy the ride. The sound of Aaron's powerful wings, pumping through the air, lulled her to sleep. She wasn't sure how long she had slept, but when she woke she was in her own room; safely tucked in bed. She lay in bed, closed her eyes and thoughts of Aaron filled her brain. She thought about their first meeting and the wonderful time they spent together. She thought about Andrea and Rachel and how lucky they were to have their father, Gunter, back with them. She thought about Shannon, Bill and Noelle and their fantastic adventure together. But most of all, she thought about how lucky she was to have such wonderful new friends. Her mind was filled with all those wonderful thoughts; they were thoughts that would last a lifetime.

On the other side of town, Chuck and Nadia were home trying there best to figure out how to repair their broken roof. The snoopy neighbors gathered to find out if Nadia knew what happened to the roof and advised them to call the insurance company.

"It's devaluating the price of our houses," one thoughtful and concerned neighbor cried out and patted Chuck roughly on the back.

Thaliana, Gunter, Andrea and Rachel sat cozily at the farm in front of a roaring fire, catching up on the time they were apart. They had asked Aaron to join them, but he declined, saying he had places to go and things to do.

Shannon had a lot of explaining to do with her parents and the police. Her parents didn't have a clue that she was a witch. Even if they did, sneaking off without telling anyone was taboo. She was going to be spending at least a month grounded to her room after it was all said and done.

Aaron spent his time sitting alone, in the icy wind, on top of Enger Tower, looking off towards Barkers Island, where he had first flown with Kyra. He sat staring into the dark, sparkling, expanse of the bay; a pit of loneliness throbbed in his heart. No one had seen his parents at Grackles cave. In fact, since their disappearance, there wasn't any information about their whereabouts, what happened to them or why.

Aaron's Grandfather had died, at the hand of Grackle, not long after he was banished. A single tear trickled down his dragon face. He still had his relatives, but he longed for his parents. The emptiness that gnawed inside him, threatened to tear him apart. He longed for the sound of their voices, the warmth of their touch and the comfort of being wrapped in their loving arms.

I'm here Aaron. Kyra's soft, sweet, voiced call out to him in his mind. *I will always be with you. As long as we have each other, we will never be alone. I will wipe away your tears and be your strength when you falter.*

Aaron wiped the tears from his eyes and warmth radiated through his body. He leapt into the frosty air, casting his sorrows aside, and danced among the moon struck sky. He was filled with hope for the future; a future overflowing with happiness; a future he would share with Kyra by his side.

Chapter 22
SCHOOL DAYS

Kyra was still sleepy when her alarm clock announced that it was time for her to get up and get ready for school. She dressed quickly and ran downstairs. Sunny was sitting in her usual spot at the table with coffee cup in hand; Kyra greeted her as she walked into the kitchen.

"Good morning," she said to her mom. "Sleep well?"

Kyra could tell by the bags under her mother's eyes that she hadn't. She wondered how long her mother had sat up explaining to her father about the hole in the wall, caused by Bigfoot, and whether or not he accepted her explanation.

"Ya," her mother replied, sleepily. "And you?"

"I slept just fine."

"Your father didn't believe me when I told him that Bigfoot made that hole in the wall."

"Dad doesn't believe in Bigfoot. He only believes in space aliens."

"Ya, your right. I should have told him that space aliens came down and, umm, decided we needed another hole."

"That's funny mom," Kyra said laughing. "If you want, I can tell him."

"No. Let him believe what he wants. A hole is a hole," Sunny said, and then she laughed.

Kyra shrugged her shoulders and smiled.

"Mom?"

"Yes dear."

"Why didn't you tell me?"

"Tell you what Kyra?"

"About being *the one*."

Her mother cast a pair of loving eyes at her and smiled warmly.

"Kyra, I never told you because I didn't want to put the burden of that much responsibility on your young shoulders. I mean, it was tough enough for you growing up without your father being around so often, and all the pressure you were under at school, I just thought it would be one less thing for you to worry about. Then too, I think it was much better you found this way and was brave enough to face it on your own. I'm so proud of you."

Kyra ran to her mother and hugged her tightly. Then she stepped back and gazed at her smiling face.

"Where did you learn to wield a sword like that?"

"Grammy taught me when I was a little girl."

"Grammy? Where did she learn to fight like that?"

"That's a long story," Sunny replied. "We'll talk about it tonight when you get home from school."

"Okay mom," Kyra said, grabbing a jacket from the closet and slipping into. "See you tonight."

She ran to the bus stop. The bus rounded the corner just as she made it to the curb. She climbed aboard the bus without a care in the world. Shannon and Noelle were in their usual seats.

"Hi!" Kyra said to the pair happily.

"Loser," the pair chanted back.

Kyra staggered past them hurt and bewilder. Someone had jammed a note into her hand. She looked around the bus trying to locate an empty seat. She was fighting back an overwhelming urge to cry. She walked to the back of the bus and fell into a seat. Then she clumsily opened the note in her hand and read it.

Dear Kyra:

No offense, but we have an image to uphold. In all honesty, we actually kind of like you. See you at your house after school. Shannon and Noelle.

The note was signed. Kyra smiled brightly. *Some things do change. One thing at a time,* she thought to herself. For the first time the bus ride to school was bearable. They all knew that together they had changed the world in their own way. Kyra wondered if Aaron would be in his wheelchair when she saw him or walking. She wondered if what had happened up north would carry on its affect and if it did why. Two words echoed in her mind, *Moon Struck.*

THE END or is it?